CARNIVORE

He wanted to scream but no sound came from his lips. His silent pleadings went unheeded. The creatures of the forest had conv...  him; waiting to atta... hurry, they had all n...

Lord Corby's voice... again. Jemmy could... crazy so that he writh... begging the beasts of... as he himself would... out of its misery.

But they let him suffer because it was decreed by the earl who had given them sanctuary within his boundaries. That was the Corby Curse.

Also in Arrow by Guy N. Smith

Accursed
Alligators
Cannibals
Deathball
Demons
The Festering
The Island
Manitou Doll
The Master

CARNIVORE

Guy N. Smith

ARROW BOOKS

Arrow Books Limited
20 Vauxhall Bridge Road, London SW1V 2SA

An imprint of Random Century Group

London Melbourne Sydney Auckland
Johannesburg and agencies throughout
the world

First published in 1990

© Guy Smith Associates 1990

The right of Guy N. Smith to be identified as the author of this work has been asserted by him in accordance with the Copyright, Designs and Patents Act, 1988

This book is sold subject to the condition that it shall not, by way of trade or otherwise be lent, resold, hired out, or otherwise circulated without the publisher's prior consent in any form of binding or cover other than that in which it is published and without a similar condition including this condition being imposed on the subsequent purchaser

Phototypeset by Input Typesetting Ltd, London

Printed and bound in Great Britain by
Courier International Ltd, Tiptree, Essex

ISBN 0 09 961090 6

For Peter Lavery
and the good old days.

PROLOGUE

Jemmy Black knew that the deer would come at twilight, regal beasts materializing like wraiths out of the winter mist on the edge of the big oak wood. There was no doubt in his mind; they had come every night for the past week whilst he had lain hidden watching them, and there was no reason to suppose that tonight would be any different. He braced himself against the bitter December cold and forced himself to be patient. The crossbow lay cocked by his side as he would not trust his numbed fingers to draw it when the moment came. He would need to be quick and sure because there would only be time for one shot, true or false. Now it was the thrill of uncertainty that brought a shiver to his lean body for his aim would mean the difference between eating and starving, maybe even living or hanging.

Once, his face had been fleshy and full, his body strong and powerful, well fed. Now it was near-skeletal beneath the ragged peasant clothes that hung pitifully from his frame, with hollowed cheeks that even his bushy black beard failed to hide and eyes that burned brightly out of sunken sockets as he stared into the misty twilight. At thirty-five he was almost toothless because his gums were diseased with undernourishment, and his hands shook so that he scarcely dared to trust them. One bolt, straight and true, that was all he asked. A beast felled stone dead, and pray God that he still had strength enough to gralloch it. His thin lips were drawn back in a perpetual grimace of hatred towards the lord of these rich lands in the heart of England where there was plenty for all, but starving serfs were denied all save turnips from the fields – food which they had to share with the deer herds, relegating them to the status of animals. On the Corby lands it was a sin punishable by death to eat life-giving meat.

In his mind Jemmy saw again the one who ruled this rich and fertile estate, which stretched back almost to the boundaries of Stratford. Astride his jet-black hunter, dressed in a velvet coat with riding trousers fashioned from the finest hide, he had an expression of arrogance on his cruel, aquiline face. He showed no kindness to humans, only towards the birds and beasts which abounded in field and forest. His small eyes glinted dangerously, madly, and made you afraid for no other reason than because you happened to be human. The Earl of Corby's father had been a huntsman well-known throughout England, and countless numbers of fleet-footed stags had finally turned at bay when the famous Corby pack cornered them. But that was almost a quarter of a century ago and things were different now. It was a bad day, indeed, that grey autumn afternoon when the old earl had passed on.

The young earl was mad. Everybody knew that. Petty obsessions became major issues and then were proclaimed law within his extensive boundaries. Once his father had horsewhipped him because he had attempted to throw the hounds off their scent by scattering hunks of venison from the cellars of the big house in the woods. The callow youth had screamed his defiance along with his pain, humiliated but undaunted. 'It is a sin to kill,' he had screeched, hands clasped to his bleeding buttocks. 'It is cannibalism to eat flesh, whether it is human or animal, but rather would I eat human meat than that of dumb, defenceless creatures. And one day, I swear to you, killing will be banned on these lands, so hear me God!'

The young man's words had sent a chill through the watching huntsmen, for they knew that the heir to these Corby lands meant every word he yelled. And there was an expression upon his pallid, pain-racked features that told them it was no empty threat. That day would come.

And at the first kill they toasted the health of their lord and master, wishing him good health and longevity.

A decade passed before the winds of change began to freshen. The new laws were proclaimed in the Corby chapel that wintry Sunday morning. The new earl took the prayers then stood to give his address. His voice shook with passion, escalating to a high pitch as he gave vent to the inner wounds that he had nursed in seething silence since that day when he was thrashed in the forest glade.

'From henceforth it is forbidden to kill.' His eyes bulged as he spoke, the veins in his forehead protruded and throbbed visibly. 'Even the rats in the ricks shall be spared because Our Lord gave them life, just as He gave it to us. And who are we to take it away? Only God can proclaim death . . . *unless, perchance, any of you are caught snaring or trapping the beasts which abound on my lands. From this day on, those who transgress will surely forfeit their own lives!*'

That was two years ago, Jemmy recalled with a grim bitterness. Two years of near-starvation, during which disease and death had ravaged the villagers. Infants died. Mothers died in childbirth because they had no stamina to withstand the rigours of bearing babies. Menfolk sickened because they had not the strength to work day after day in the fields. Yet in all other matters the young lord was generous. There was firewood aplenty for the gathering in the forests, crops from the fields. But it was not just the lack of meat, it was the absence of hides from which to make warm clothes for the bitter winters.

And even the deer were beginning to sicken. Without the cull which removed the weak and diseased from their midst, they, too, were suffering. Jemmy shook his head with sadness, for in another decade all that would remain would be the predators. Then they would begin to prey on one another. Only the rats seemed unaffected, swarming in the granaries, eating and fouling the grain, spreading disease from which man had lost his immunity.

For himself, Jemmy did not care. It was for Mary and her unborn child, and for Richard and Elizabeth, neither of them yet ten years old, for whom he would kill a stag. He would risk his life this night, for without fresh meat they would all surely die. He had no choice.

He sensed a movement on the edge of the forest before he actually made out the shape of a deer. Now two, three . . . four. Regal creatures which moved with a dignity and alertness other beasts were denied. A stag, the king of the forest, surely, moved forward until it was no longer a mere silhouette against the darkening background. Its coat was a brownish grey, the underparts a contrasting white. Its branching antlers, fearsome weapons of death and destruction at the rutting stand, crowned a head held proudly aloft as it sniffed the air for signs of danger. These noble beasts of the chase were unaccustomed to not being hunted; it was as though even they felt it an unnatural state of affairs and would rather have died swiftly than sickened and lingered.

Jemmy stiffened but did not move. Perhaps the stag sensed his presence with an age-old awareness of danger that transcended eyesight and scent, for it surely could not see him lying here in the undergrowth, nor smell him, as the frosty breeze blew from the animals and towards himself. His bony fingers trembled on the crossbow but he did not lift it. A moment of doubt, of fear, but he dispelled it at once. His family depended upon his skill as a hunter; he would not fail them. Perhaps it would have been easier to snare a rabbit. No, there was not sufficient flesh on a coney to warrant the risk. Far better to be hanged for a deer than a rabbit.

The stag stood motionless, the hinds crowding in behind him. Head still raised, it scented until it was satisfied that all was safe, and only then did it permit its female followers to begin to graze the frosted turnip tops. It did not join them but remained there on guard, a silent sentry who would warn them at the first hint of danger.

Slowly Jemmy raised his crossbow and brought it up to his shoulder. One deadly bolt; he did not possess another because there would be no second attempt. Its head had been fashioned on the smithy's forge where he worked. The bow itself was a forbidden weapon, for the earl's keepers had confiscated all peasant weaponry the week after the proclamation of the new law. Jemmy had kept his crossbow hidden in an old badger sett, wrapped in rotting hessian, well greased so that it might function to perfection on the first occasion it was needed.

His hands shook; he had difficulty in taking a sight. The crossbow wavered, but with a supreme mental and physical effort he steadied it. The neck; he knew he would not miss, convinced himself of it, recalled those nights in the old days when he and old Jeb the cartwright had poached forbidden venison beneath a full moon. It was no different now: the well-prepared ambush, the careful shot, a beast falling and kicking its last, the rest fleeing with a drumming of hooves on the ferny floor. In that instant he heard and felt the bolt go, a missile of death hurtling to its mark faster than the eye could follow. There was a soft thud, and he let out his pent-up breath in relief as he saw the stag stumble.

It went down, did not even writhe its last, just lay still and huddled on the hard ground. Jemmy was aware that the other deer had fled but he was not listening to their receding hoofbeats. He was aghast, and then euphoric at what he had done. He had not missed; he knew he would not for he had been taught his marksmanship by Jeb, the King of the Poachers, as the villagers called the old man.

He crawled forward. He did not rise to his feet for the die was cast and there was no going back. He had sinned, and if he was caught by the earl's foresters then the penalty was death. Jemmy trembled, stretched out a hand and felt the warm hair of the dead stag. It was real enough, it was no fevered dream in a sweat-soaked sickbed. Mary and the children would eat. Nay, *feast*! There was enough flesh to last them a month and then . . . he would forge another bolt and kill again.

He slid his huge skinning knife out of its sheath. The wide blade was sharp. Again Jemmy had learned his craft well. The beast would be cut up, jointed, and hidden in the loft of his hovel. Its skin would be sewn into a garment to warm them all secretly on bitter nights. Lord Corby would never know, would not even suspect.

He worked fast, and for the first time that night he forgot the cold. Dusk became darkness but he did not need to see. Succulent joints of venison were piled by the sack he had brought with him, the hide rolled up. The smell of fresh meat made him heady; he could have feasted on it raw. No, within the hour the first joint would be cooking in the blackened pot over the fire and they would go to bed with full stomachs. For the first time for two years.

He was finished; it would require two, perhaps three, journeys to transport the meat back to his cottage. He would have to hurry in case the scent of freshly killed meat brought the carnivorous beasts of the forest to his cache whilst he was away. He was sweating as he swung the full sack up on to his shoulder. And it was at that instant that rough hands reached out of the darkness for him and a clenched fist felled him to the ground.

A few seconds of blackness, and then he was blinded by the glare of a lantern. Cruel fingers dug into his wasted flesh. There was an arm around his neck almost throttling him. He saw moving shapes, which became men as they crowded into the circle of light cast by the lamp, men with wide-brimmed hats and thick-knitted tunics. Foresters, formerly gamekeepers in the old earl's day, with swarthy features that leered and showed no mercy.

'Why, if it isn't old Jemmy!' Mock surprise; a heavy boot thumped into his ribs and winded him. 'And I suppose ye found the stag dead and jointed and were just about to bring it down for the earl hisself to see!' Guffaws; another boot drove into Jemmy's side.

They had ropes, and at first he thought that they were going to hang him right there, leaving his dangling body for the crows to feed on at first light. Groping hands again tore at his clothing, ribboning the rotting material so that it shredded from his body. He felt the icy night air on his nakedness, and shivered with cold and terror.

'Thou shalt not kill, Jemmy, and the penalty is death!'

They dragged his backwards, slammed him up against the bole of a giant oak on the edge of the wood, and held him upright so that the gnarled trunk scraped his back. He felt the ropes begin to cut deep into his skin, pulling him tight against the tree. They bound him securely around his torso, pinioning his arms, then his loins and his ankles. Already parts of him were becoming numb as his circulation was restricted.

The cold was terrible now, eating into him, his bonds seemed to restrict his shivering. Except his teeth; he heard them clacking loudly. And somewhere close by, a horse's hooves were scraping on the hard, frosty ground. Another lantern, another rider. The newcomer dismounted, and Jemmy saw the outline of a cloaked man. His worst fears were confirmed as the foresters stood respectfully to one side. Lord Corby had arrived!

The earl's face was shadowed by the wide brim of his hat, but his tall figure bespoke gloating and cruelty, as if to say: *I'm delighted you've slain a stag, peasant, because now I can slay you!* His eyes glowed evilly, twin pinpoints in the darkness 'The first one!' A guttural whisper. 'The first to die.'

Jemmy did not answer, just stared into that shadowed

face, and his only fear was for his wife and children. Do as you will with me, he thought, but spare my family. You have no right to deny them meat.

'Truly the beast of the chase, defenceless and praying for death.' Corby's tone was shrill; there was no mistaking his madness. 'Now you know how a hunted stag feels, peasant. But the stag is more fortunate. At least, its end was *reasonably* swift. Yours will not be!'

Jemmy was aware of how even the watching foresters shrank back. They had expected, perhaps, the victim's execution by sword or knife. Instead...

'You will remain here, just as you are' – the earl's tone was low, scarcely audible, as though even he was afraid of the sentence he had passed upon this poacher – 'naked and defenceless. You will die, certainly before morning. Exposure, the elements, perhaps. Who knows what fate will befall one left in the forest all night. Wolves, maybe – there are still odd ones, even in these parts. Or night owls come to feed on human eyes, in which case you will be spared the sight of your attackers. None the less, you will die in the knowledge that you have killed. *And may the Corby Curse be upon you and your kind who slaughter God's creatures, from this day on. May your fate be that of others who defy my law, for all time!*'

Then they were gone, and Jemmy was left alone, cringing in the icy blackness of a December night, shivering and moaning softly, trying to stop his teeth clattering in case the noise attracted... *something*.

He gave up straining at his bonds, for without assistance he could not possibly free himself. He contemplated shouting for help, but even if somebody heard him they would be afraid to defy the earl and free him. And *something else* might hear him.

A numbness slowly enveloped him that was not wholly brought on by a lack of circulating blood. The coldness reached a peak and left him, a naked wretched being whose only thought was for his family. And even thinking was becoming difficult, as if some kind of balm had been administered to alleviate his suffering. He had no conception of time; he was in a dark void where he would remain forever. Perhaps this was the hell with which one was threatened in church.

Slowly came the awareness that he was no longer alone. Faint movements around him, a rustling of the frosty grasses, scrapings on the hard ground. He stared into the blackness, anticipating the blinding glare of a lantern, surely the foresters had returned to set him free. You have learned your lesson this time, Jemmy, they would say. Next time we shall hang you. But there was no welcoming light, just stealthy movements all around him.

Then he saw the eyes, a myriad of luminous orbs, a semicircle of them just staring at him. He felt the sheer hatred of those animal expressions, the way they burned their message into him: *Now you know how a hunted beast feels, Jemmy Black. The fear, the knowledge that you are going to die. Sooner or later.*

He smelled their fetid odours, the stench of wild beasts emerging from their stinking lairs, then began to feel the coldness again. He wanted to scream but no sound came from his lips. His silent pleadings went unheeded. The creatures of the forest had converged here to mock him, to taunt him; waiting to attack, to savage him. There was no hurry, they had all night.

Lord Corby's voice echoed in his brain, over and over again. Jemmy could not dispel it. It was driving him crazy so that he writhed in his bonds, screaming mutely, begging the beasts of the night to despatch him swiftly, as he himself would finish off a wounded stag to put it out of its misery.

But they let him suffer because it was decreed by the earl who had given them sanctuary within his boundaries. That was the Corby Curse.

1

Sir Thomas Corby had witnessed the decline of his family's fortune over the past eighteen months. The rot had begun with the stock market crash a year last October, which had wiped a good quarter of a million off his holdings. That was bad enough, but he had had a premonition that it was only the beginning. He had known his ex-wife Danielle would be making a claim on him, but never in his wildest dreams had he thought that a judge would grant her a lump sum of three quarters of a million pounds. The bastard! And she was a bloody bitch, screwing on the side whilst he was having an affair with Alexis Innerman, the TV presenter. His affair had come to light, but Danielle's had not, until afterwards, when it did not really matter. One law for women and another for men! He had begun hitting the bottle again when there was no alternative but to begin selling off land, and land prices had slumped abysmally.

The home farm went first, in three lots. It did not make the reserve at auction, and in desperation he accepted offers. That kept his creditors at bay – for a while. But when you are on the downhill slide nothing goes right for you. He came to that conclusion the following spring. He opened the big house to the public, but nobody seemed interested – a trickle of tourists at weekends, virtually nobody on weekdays. Because Stratford was too close; they queued for the Bard's birthplace, but nobody bothered about the Corby home. Christ, his ancestor had owned half the surrounding countryside two centuries ago and nobody even remembered his name! The present Lord Corby had invested a fortune speculating on tourism. He had had the house restored to its former state and glossy brochures printed, the majority of which were still stacked in the cupboard in the entrance hall.

Maybe he had gone about it the wrong way, Corby thought, and should have opened a wildlife park like his rivals. But it was too late now; the bank was pushing him to the brink. Finally he put the house and the remaining five hundred hectares of arable land up for sale. The estate agents were confident of getting a million and a half for it. That was six months ago. There had been a string of viewers but no offers; now it was up for just over a million and a quarter, and at long last they had somebody in with an offer. An *offer*! The bloody cheek of it. It was a cut-price bargain to begin with, and the prospective buyer was even now trying to impose conditions on the sale. Sod him, he wanted that two-hundred-year-old clause forbidding the killing of wild animals removed from the deeds!

Sir Thomas Corby was approaching his fiftieth birthday, and for the first time in his life he accepted that he looked his age; his hair was greying, those lines on his features were more pronounced. He preferred to call it a lived-in face rather than an ageing one. Craggy, weatherbeaten, anything except ageing. He had lost a stone in weight, and had ceased trying to convince himself that he had been attempting to reduce his waistline for years. He had not needed to. He was gaunt. His shoulders were stooped, due to a loss of confidence; humiliation. One could only put on an act for so long. When the chips were down, one had to face up to it. Three double whiskies between a late breakfast and an early lunch were not helping. And if he was unlucky enough to get stopped by the police on the drive into town, then that would just add insult to the injuries which had gone before. Suddenly he did not care any more. Get the Corby estate sold, and there should be enough left over to allow him to start afresh somewhere else and live reasonably comfortably for the rest of his life. He would go abroad, of course. But first, he had to sell the last of his estate.

He felt numbed, philosophical, and just went along with events – until he scraped the side of his Mercedes against a concrete pillar in the multi-storey car park. Bloody careless, don't try and excuse yourself that you're bogged down with worry, he told himself. Look on the bright side; it might have been somebody else's car and the owner could have called the police. All the same, his mood was changing to one of anger. I'm giving the place away and still this bugger Broughton isn't satisfied, he thought. And Huwyl Jones, the solicitor, wasn't helping by saying that if you paid the piper you called the tune. *I'm not the bloody piper*! This looked like being a stormy meeting in Jones's office; the three of them – the lawyer, Broughton and himself. It wasn't necessary, vendor and purchaser should conduct their haggle via their respective lawyers, Corby thought. But he was desperate to sell and there was only one offer on the table. If that fell through, then he'd go to the wall; and if the bank foreclosed, then there might not be much left over in the kitty afterwards. If anything. He contemplated calling in somewhere for another double Scotch but there wasn't time. He was five minutes late already. But weren't titled people expected to be late? However, he didn't bother with the whisky.

'Ah, Sir Thomas, allow me to introduce you to John Broughton, owner of Broughton Safaris, the well-known sporting agency.' Huwyl Jones was nervous. He reminded Corby of a typical butler, and he almost looked to see if the solicitor had a napkin folded over one arm and a silver salver in his hand. Over polite, patronizing, but underneath it all as shrewd as they came, already totting up his legal fees.

'I'm delighted to meet you, Sir Thomas.' The handshake was firm, the voice cultured. Corby looked up into the face of a man younger than himself, more handsome than himself. His tasteful tweed suit befitted a country landowner, a gentleman farmer whose only work on the land was inspecting his domain from the comfort of a Range Rover. Educated at Eton and Cambridge, doubtless. The nouveau landed gentry, made his money elsewhere and was looking for a country estate as a status symbol. No more than thirty five at the outside, powerfully built, sure of himself. Too bloody sure for Corby's liking. For once, he felt at a distinct disadvantage, because now *he* was the pauper and this man was after the Corby estate, the family home. Christ Alive, he could almost visualize his ancestors writhing in their tombs in the vault beneath the chapel! *He* was the end of the line, the one who was giving it all away. But he was determined to make one last attempt to salvage his pride. This cocky bugger wasn't going to have it *all* his own way!

Jones was back behind his desk, hiding his nervousness in a sheaf of legal documents, rustling the papers and clearing his throat. He plucked up courage to say what he had to. 'Sir Thomas . . . you will, I am sure, recall the clause in these documents which was transcribed from the laws introduced by the Earl of Corby in 1780?' He was waiting for an answer, passing the buck. Tell this jumped-up squirt yourself, Corby thought.

'You mean the one about the prohibition of the killing of animals and livestock?' Which was why Corby had never been able to let the shooting and fishing rights, and had turned his back on valuable income in this age of chequebook sport. He had wanted it written out of the deeds; but Huwyl Jones had said it wasn't possible, mainly because Danielle was an anti-bloodsport nutter. She'd had a say then, but not any longer – because she'd been paid off.

'That's the one.' The solicitor launched into a monotone reading of the old-English phraseology.

Corby resisted the temptation to yawn. Why not just

say that you can't kill *anything* on the Corby estate and have done with it? But lawyers were long-winded, partly to impress and partly so that you did not pick holes in their findings. Jones finished, and his humourless features became visible over the top of the document.

'Mr Broughton is prepared to pay the reduced asking price if this proviso is deleted from the deeds, Sir Thomas.' The documents were rustled, then raised again to create a hiding place for the embarrassed solicitor.

'Is that so, Mr Broughton?' Corby turned to him, hoping that he had got his disdainful expression right.

'That's so, Sir Thomas.' Arrogant bastard, Corby thought. 'You see, my company, Broughton Safaris, arranges virtually every type of shooting for our clients all over the world. We have wild-boar shooting in Germany, pheasant shooting in Hungary, partridges in Spain, but the fact of the matter is that sportsmen from abroad will pay the earth for traditional English sport. Hence, I would like to develop the potential of the Corby estate and at the same time live there with my wife.'

'And if you anticipate making a bloody fortune out of *my* ancestral home, then why are you trying to knock me down on the price?'

'I have to allow for the investment necessary to make the estate what I want it to be. Believe me, Sir Thomas, it will cost an arm and a leg before the first shot is even fired.'

'Don't you think shooting is rather cruel and unnecessary?' Sir Thomas hoped that his ancestor in his tomb might hear this sop to appease the dead. He wouldn't give in easily.

'I can't see how that issue figures in our dealings.' Broughton's reply was clipped, abrupt. 'Fieldsports are a matter of personal conscience, sir, but in this instance we are talking about whether I buy or not. Without the sporting rights, I most certainly will not. I must make that quite clear.'

'My ancestor made that law on his lands, and who am I to change it?' There was a slight flush on Corby's cheeks. 'Anyway, I don't think it can be done.'

Jones cleared his throat again and peeped over the edge of the yellowing sheets of paper secured with a red ribbon. He looked from Corby to Broughton, then back again to his client, as if to say: *You'll* have to ask me that, Sir Thomas, I'm not volunteering the information.

'It *can't* be done, can it, Jones?'

'That rests with you entirely, Sir Thomas.' The voice quavered slightly. 'You are the sole owner, mortgaged to the bank, of course. The decision is yours as to whether or not wildlife can be killed on your lands. An affidavit reversing the 1780 proclamation of a sanctuary can be added upon your sole instructions. I shall be pleased to carry out your instructions, whatever you decide.'

Blast you, Jones, you've put the ball back in my court when you could just as easily have said it couldn't be done! Corby pursed his lips and looked up at the ceiling. He spied a cobweb in a dusty corner. A fly trapped in it was buzzing its fear. Caught, like me, he thought. Damn it, why should I pronounce the death sentence on the wildlife that abounds in the park – the deer, hares, rabbits . . . the wild duck on the lake? The old boy was right two centuries ago. He made the ruling out of kindness. It's not for me to repeal a local law. I have the power to, though. *Power*. Any power I have will be gone the moment I concede this issue. Broughton's got power over me. No, he hasn't, I'm still the Corby landowner. But not for long, either way. They were both waiting for him; he could hear their breathing quicken. Don't try to push me, he warned silently. The bank's pushing me. Once they foreclose and sell the estate, anything might happen to it. Just anything.

Broughton might bide his time and buy from the bank, cheaper. The gloating bastard! Like that spider up there, he had woven his web.

'Perhaps we can find a compromise, Mr Broughton.' It sounded weak. Corby scarcely recognized his own voice.

'What kind of a compromise?'

Corby tried to look at the solicitor again but the documents were screening him. It's *your* decision, Sir Thomas, was the unspoken message. Concede and sell, take your money and run. Or else the bank will.

'I'd like time to think it over.'

Silence. They were both looking at him now. He experienced pressure, unspoken ultimatums.

'How long, Sir Thomas?' Broughton sounded tired, bored. 'I do have another place in mind. I've made a provisional appointment to view and meet the vendors tomorrow. Brackley Park.'

Corby felt himself begin to sweat. Broughton might be bluffing but he had got his facts right. Brackley Park, less than five miles away, had just been put on the market – and it was two hundred thousand cheaper. Not so prestigious, but doubtless the sporting side did not have any strings attached. He sighed, and closed his eyes momentarily. I've fought you every inch of the way but you've won in the end, he thought.

'All right,' He opened his eyes and looked down at the fraying carpet, another part of legal tradition. 'I'll sign an affidavit if you'll draw it up, Jones.'

Corby sensed Broughton's triumph, hated himself for what he had done and made a silent apology to the bones of his distant ancestor.

Corby needed that whisky now, more than he had ever needed one, in his desire, his craving, to obliterate from his memory what he had done. He merged with the lunchtime businessmen drinkers in the hotel lounge, trying to submerge his identity and drown it in a double malt. Then a second one, not just because he needed it but because he did not want to return home. I don't have a home, he remembered. I've just signed it away – and an age-old tradition with it. I've sounded the death knell on God's creatures, those roe deer which graze on the big lawn and nibble the rose bushes. Hordes of trigger-happy foreigners will slaughter them and the blood will be on my hands. He thought about going back to the lawyer's and reversing his decision. It wouldn't do any good, there was no alternative. He had just made it easy for the bastards.

He caught the side of the car on that concrete stanchion again on the way out and heard the screech of metallic pain. It didn't matter a damn, nothing did. Tonight he would get drunk. Really drunk.

The Mercedes would have to go, of course. Because it belonged to the estate, it wasn't his personally. Maybe it would go in the farm implements sale. He laughed aloud at the thought. No matter, cars were cars, whatever their make, just hunks of tin sheeting that came in different shapes and sizes. Some had more powerful engines than others, that was the only difference, enabling you to go faster. He was doing ninety five now, and pushed his foot down still harder. Give her a real burn-up, he thought, just one last time, see what she'll do flat out.

He hit the dual carriageway; five miles to the turn-off for Corby village. Mental calculations; he was doing a ton now . . . 100 miles in an hour, 50 in half an hour . . . 25 in a quarter . . . 12½ in 7½ minutes. Getting a bit complicated. About three minutes, then. Give her all you've got, Tommy.

Christ, she was juddering. He hoped it wasn't a slow puncture. No, it wasn't likely because only last week he'd had a new set of tyres fitted. Probably the wheels hadn't been balanced. Lazy bastards, he'd give them a bollocking if that was the case. You couldn't trust these garages, they ripped you off and did a shoddy job into the bargain.

The lanes were busy, he had to slow as he caught up with a Rover. *Get into the nearside, you creeping bastard*! It was as if the other driver had heard him; he indicated and pulled in between a lorry and a car. Corby surged forward again and felt the steering wheel vibrating in his hands, an unpleasant experience. Only about another minute before he came to the Corby sign. But he wasn't slowing down yet.

It was starting to drizzle. A thin film of opaqueness on the windscreen obstructed his vision. He flicked the wipers on. They smeared on the windscreen, squeaking. The sound was as annoying as that shuddering of the wheels. Damn it, he wouldn't turn off, he'd carry right on into Birmingham and sort that fucking garage out!

A line of slow cars, not one of them was exceeding seventy! He put his headlights on, full beam. There was spray now, filth in the drizzle. He pushed the washer button. Nothing. Oh, for fuck's sake! The Mercedes was supposed to have been serviced as well as having the tyres changed. They hadn't done a bloody thing, just fitted a new set of Michelins and charged him the best part of three hundred quid. *Right, you buggers, here I come*!

The Mercedes swerved to the left. A lorry blared its horn and he swung the wheel hard over. The car came back into the offside lane and almost caught the central reservation kerb. Christ! His heart flipped. He fought to control the vehicle but it was swerving like a bucking steer trying to get its head and throw its rider.

Lights were flashing behind him, more horns wailing. Scared. He was scared to hell. Corby took his foot right off the throttle, and saw that he was too close to the Capri in front. He braked hard, then felt the Mercedes slewing to the right.

No! Too late, he saw the central reservation with its concrete base and long grassy mound, and knew there was no way he could avoid hitting it. A bump, then the bonnet was vertical. He saw grey clouds through a dirty film, a lowering sky as if he was piloting a light aircraft and taking off. Now airborne with nothing beneath the wheels, he closed his eyes because he did not want to see.

Dipping, nose-diving; the underside struck something. He heard it tearing, and clung grimly to the wheel. Sideways on, a gigantic monster with angry eyes was bearing down upon him, hungry for him, its gaping gridded mouth eager to devour him. Knowing that there was no hope, he accepted his fate.

Seconds seemed hours before the final impact, during which he was aware of a voice inside his head, senile rasping tones that were far more terrifying than the speeding articulated lorry that had singled him out for the victim of its wrath.

'Those who kill the wild animals which abound on my lands shall forfeit their own lives from this day on!'

And in those few terrible seconds before he died, Sir Thomas knew that the Corby Curse was no myth; that it had lived on over the centuries since his ancestor proclaimed his lands a sanctuary for wildlife; that it was still alive, and those who broke the law would die. And the last of the Corbys was the first victim.

2

Pamela Broughton had never relished the idea of country life. It was a silly fashion that some people thought was a kind of status symbol which impressed others. In effect it was primitive; you made life unnecessarily hard for yourself. Who, in their right mind, wanted all the work involved in cutting up wood and laboriously stoking some smoky woodburner that stank the house out, when you could have thermostatically controlled heating at the flick of a switch? Masochism, that was what it was, trying to create an image, kidding yourself that you enjoyed it. Well, if others wanted to do that, then it was fine by her; but she was quite content with their Mayfair penthouse.

Fair enough, it was John's line of business. Without it, they would not have everything they had. But in the beginning it was something distant, she never actually came into contact with it. He booked these safaris and shooting expeditions and was often away, mostly abroad, for weeks at a time. She didn't mind because she had her own social circle and was never bored. Once he had offered to take her on one of these trips, camping out in Tunisia whilst the party spent their days hunting some poor defenceless animals. She didn't mind them doing that but she was damned if she was going to be their head cook and bottle-washer, because that was what it would end up as; a woman was just *too* convenient to have around. And, anyway, there would be hordes of mosquitoes, perhaps poisonous snakes, and God alone knew what else. You carry on, dear, and don't mind me, she'd told him. When you go on a world cruise or something *civilized*, then I'll be only too happy to accompany you. In the meantime, London and our annual fortnight in the Bahamas will suit me down to the ground.

Then he had talked about buying a country estate, a sixteen-bedroomed mansion. It sounded idyllic; there would be a staff of servants to run the place and see to all the cooking and household chores. She would enjoy a life of luxury, and Stratford-on-Avon was certainly a prestigious address. London wasn't far away, just down the road really – she had read an article somewhere about businessmen who worked in London and lived in Stratford, commuting daily. Pamela decided she could enjoy the best of both worlds. But now she was disillusioned and angry. John had misled her, it was a downright bloody deception!

For a start, Corby House was not *in* Stratford, it was several miles away, buried in the wilderness of the so-called Heart of England. It was a good half-mile from the main road, down a bumpy track that badly needed resurfacing. The house itself would have to have a lot of work done on it. It had fallen into a state of disrepair, apart from one section which had been renovated for a public viewing enterprise by the previous owner, and the scheme had proved an unmitigated failure. No wonder; it was no stately home, just a big old draughty house. John said not to worry, he had arranged for the builders to start work next month. Next month! And in the meantime she had to live here! Footsteps echoed, the whole place was spooky. Well, he'd better get a move on and have it rendered *habitable* before next winter. He was already interviewing staff, he had engaged two gardeners. Blow the garden! She didn't give a damn about what was outside Corby House, it was the *inside* that mattered. And until he employed some kitchen staff he could bloody well get his own meals, because she wasn't going to allow herself to be indoctrinated into a domestic role. In the meantime she would eat out. John's priority seemed to be finding a *gamekeeper*. He was supposed to be coming home to interview one this evening. It was late March now, and a lot of things had to change by July; she had a self-imposed time-limit of four months on a change for the better, as she had told her husband only the other night.

She studied her reflection in the full-length bedroom mirror. Slim, tall, attractive, nobody could deny her that. Her long dark hair fell below her shoulders. She toyed with it, wondering how she would look if she changed her fashionable long dress for a two-piece tweed suit. Or slummed it and wore jeans and a sweater like most of those yuppy wives did. Ugh! No, she wasn't trading her personality for that of a country bumpkin lady of the manor. *If* she remained here, then she wasn't making any changes. As for a social life, hers was still in London and she anticipated spending a lot of time away from home. Not for her, coffee mornings, wine and cheese parties and the Women's Institute, or any of those traditional boring country gatherings.

She stood in the window, looking down on the weedy gravel drive and the dense shrubbery screening the surrounding countryside. Those rhododendrons might look fine in flower, but for the rest of the year all they did was create an atmosphere of claustrophobia. She would have a word with those gardener chaps tomorrow and see about having the bushes cut down to let some light in. Her car glinted in the afternoon sunshine, a red Justy. Four-wheel drive; it was a disturbing thought, a hint of mud and snow. She was definitely going to spend the winters in London, and John had better get used to the idea. They might be snowed in here for weeks!

Last night had been a trauma, but she had changed her mind about confiding in her husband. A man who spent weeks out in the veldt with hunting parties would only scoff at her fears in the English countryside. Nevertheless, it *had* been disturbing. With darkness, her loneliness had merged into unease . . . John was away overnight, she was here all alone, not so much as a maid sleeping in the servants' quarters. What did one do in the case of an emergency? There was always the telephone. First she experienced the need to talk to somebody, just frivolous chatter, so she decided to ring Stephanie in Mayfair. That was when Pamela discovered the phone was dead! Merciful God, she almost rushed out to the car and drove right out of there! Either the telephone was out of order, or else the engineers had not reconnected the line yet. It gave her a sense of abandonment, a trapped feeling. She switched on all the lights in the upper storey, but couldn't settle to anything. She wasn't a keen reader, television bored her, and this wasn't London, where you could fix up a social evening with a quick phone call. Here the telephone wasn't even working!

So she retired just after ten o'clock, switched off those surplus lights and hastened up to her bedroom. At least the lock on the door functioned! She undressed, climbed into bed and, with some reluctance, plunged the room into darkness. Except that it was not really dark because there was a full moon outside, which penetrated the curtains with its ghostly glow, creating eerie shadows. You're being stupid, she told herself, it's never properly dark in London. But in the metropolis the night light was created by streetlamps, the headlights of never-ceasing traffic in the road below. That was different, there were people all around; here there was nobody.

Noises. She lay listening to them, and tried to work out for her own peace of mind what they were. All old houses creaked in the night – warped floorboards. Not in London, though. In the city it was never quiet, there were innumerable explicable sounds all around to mask the arthritic groans of historic houses. The noises were there, just as they were in Corby House, but you didn't hear them. She felt a little easier after coming to that conclusion. But you did not hear *animal* sounds in London!

Pamela tensed. Her mouth was dry, and she was aware of the quickening of her heartbeat. The fluttering, constantly shifting noise wasn't the wind because it was still night. *Birds*! She almost voiced her relief aloud as the answer came to her. Those dense bushes outside were probably full of roosting birds, every imaginable species seeking a safe place in their leafy foliage for the nocturnal hours. In the city she was sometimes troubled by feral pigeons roosting on the roof and the window-sills, fouling the stonework with their droppings. If they became too much of a nuisance she telephoned the council and they discreetly arranged for their pest officer to remove the birds; he usually put down some kind of narcotic poison and she wasn't bothered again for a while. Tomorrow she would phone the council and . . . except that the bloody telephone wasn't working. The new gardeners then, they could attend to it. The remedy was quite simple: cut down the shrubs, and there would be nowhere for those awful feathered creatures to sleep. They would have to go and find some field hedgerows or a wood. But why did they keep moving about, why didn't they go to sleep? It was the moonlight, she decided. They couldn't make up their minds whether it was night or day.

There was another rustling outside, but it was somehow different. She held her breath and listened again. It wasn't like the flapping of tiny wings, rather a heavier sound – branches being pushed to one side to allow some heavier creature to pass through. She thought she heard a grunt, just once. And then there was silence except for the birds. A badger, perhaps, or a fox after the birds. She hoped it was a fox; it might solve her problem. *Go on, Basil, eat them or frighten them away!* She tried to laugh at her own joke but it really wasn't very funny, not when she was all alone, miles from civilization and there wasn't even a telephone.

Without warning something screamed. A piercing, almost human screech shattered the uneasy stillness of a rural night, a penetrating sound that rose to a terrifying pitch, vibrating the atmosphere, from directly beneath the bedroom window.

Pamela Broughton almost screamed with it. She sat upright in the bed, glancing about her as though she expected to find some awful creature lurking in the shadows. Oh, God, whatever was it! An animal of some kind? She fought to convince herself that it could not possibly be human. A beast of the night – but there were no dangerous wild animals left in England these days. The last wolf had been killed over a hundred years ago. But whatever creature it was down there on the drive, it could not possibly get to her. She was safe. Wasn't she?

An escapee from a zoo? The thought came to plague her that a ferocious animal was on the loose. There was a wildlife park fairly near here, she remembered seeing a poster somewhere. A lion, a tiger, a man-eater from some jungle species! She moaned softly with terror. But even if it was a big cat it could not reach her; these upper windows were too high for even the most powerful and agile of felines. Weren't they?

Now she could hear it walking about below, the scuffling of stones, a crunching of gravel. Going away; coming back; stopping. She even thought she could hear its laboured breathing. *Get a grip on yourself, girl.*

She decided to go and take a look outside. From the safety of a locked bedroom window, of course. It was a kind of compulsion, a masochistic curiosity. She was trembling. Aware how her legs shook as she swung her feet to the floor, she wondered if they would bear her weight when she stood up. Moving towards that moonlit bow window a step at a time, she paused to listen every other pace, almost turning back once. Pull the sheets up over your head and wait for morning, she told herself. But that overpowering curiosity drove her on.

Her shaking fingers pulled a gap in the curtains, and she was amazed how light it was out there. Everywhere was bathed in an ethereal glow, a silvery, shadowy world where a thousand beasts of the night could skulk unseen. Waiting. For her. But I'm not going outside, she decided, even in the morning I'll wait until somebody comes.

The driveway was deserted. But the shadows from the surrounding shrubbery created a mysterious dark area where it was impossible to discern anything. She was still watching with frightened eyes. There's nothing out there after all, she concluded. There never had been. It was some kind of bird in that roost. A noisy one; she had no idea what species, but perhaps there were birds that screeched and ... *something was moving out of the shadows into a patch of moonlight!*

A dog! She forced relief, trying to make herself believe that it was a canine creature because dogs generally were harmless. A stray, half-starved, howling for food. But I'm not going outside to feed it, she thought.

No, it wasn't a dog. Even she had to admit that, no matter how hard she tried to convince herself otherwise. The right shape, and breeds varied in size, but the tail was wrong, long and bushy, swishing from side to side as if it was sweeping the drive. Stealthy, a hunting animal. A predator! A moonbeam washed over it, turning its coat silver then black again. It was coming towards the house, purposefully. That was what was so terrifying about it.

She anticipated its second scream even before the nerve-shattering sound hit her with the force of an electric shockwave. Its head was thrown back, the sharp features elevated so that it was looking directly up at the window. Moonlight was reflected in its eyes, twin orbs that flashed evilly. *And saw her.*

'It's a ... fox!' The whisper that began as relief changed to terror again for there was no mistaking the sheer evil that blazed from the vulpine eyes. Jaws agape, it was snarling viciously up at her, tensing as though it was about to hurl itself into the air in a leap which would carry it up to the second storey of Corby House, its weight smashing the glass. A crazed animal intent on ravaging human flesh, a nocturnal creature that embodied the hate of a hunted species for its hunters.

I'm against fox-hunting, a tiny frightened voice inside her whined pitifully. The fox halted, still watching her. She wanted to step back, let the curtain fall into place, shut it out. But she was unable to move, hypnotized by those awful hate-filled eyes. She braced herself for another scream from below. But it never came. One moment the fox was down there staring up at her, the next it was gone, as though it had never been but was all a trick of the moonlight. Except that she knew it was no mirage, not even her frightened imagination playing cruel tricks on her. There *had* been a fox down there, and there was no mistaking its malevolence. Its hate-filled screams still echoed in her brain.

She was trembling violently as she made her way back to the bed and switched the light on. She would let it burn all night; hadn't primitive man lit fires at the mouth of his cave to keep wild beasts away? She felt easier with the light on, but dawn was beginning to lighten the eastern sky before she finally fell into a troubled slumber.

That had been last night, she reminded herself as she stood looking down on the drive in the afternoon sunlight. But night would come again. Those damned gardeners had not showed up, otherwise she would have instructed them to start slashing down the rhododendrons. Probably they were working away on some part of the estate on John's instructions. She had made her mind up that she wasn't staying here another night on her own. If her husband had not showed up by dusk, then she would drive to Stratford, book in at an hotel, and stay there until he returned home. But he had to come because that fellow was arriving at six to be interviewed for the gamekeeper's job.

And then she heard a car approaching, coming down the winding track from the main road, slowing on the sharp bend beyond the wall of shrubs. She prayed that it was a dark red Subaru estate, the larger cousin of her own Justy parked down there. It was.

Gordon Shank was small and lithe, his alertness and eagerness showing in his clear blue eyes and the way he noted everything that went on around him, missing nothing. Sunburned, an outdoor man of few words, he was dressed in an open-necked checked shirt and cords, and surveying the landscape around him as the Subaru bumped across a rough grass field.

'There's some useful woodland here,' John Broughton said as he drove. 'Three good coverts and about a dozen spinneys. The farming's let, and there will be plenty of roots to hold the birds. The lie of the land, those sloping fields, gives scope for putting some high birds over the guns if they're driven right. We want to rear about four thousand birds a year, but to start with we'll have to buy in six-week-old poults. I'm afraid it's a bit of a rushed job, starting from scratch to be ready for the coming season. You'll have some help, of course – a couple of part-timers to help you put up release pens.' Broughton had already made up his mind that this was the man for the job. He had a good reference from his previous employer, and he had worked single-handed before and knew his trade. 'What do you think?'

'It's a good set-up, there's certainly potential.' There was a note of wariness in Shank's voice.

'But you see problems?'

'Keepering's never without problems.' Shank smiled wanly. 'But this estate has never been keepered before. The vermin rule the roost. Look at that rookery over there. It'll have to be thinned out. And no doubt the woods are alive with foxes. I'll have to thin them out if the pheasants are to stand any chance at all.'

'Good. I'll back you all the way, and in case you're worried about this being hunting country, forget it. The hunt will be welcome here, provided they ask permission to come and don't try to ride roughshod over us, but you don't have to save any foxes for them!'

'Fine,' the keeper grinned. 'I'll need a few score of fox snares then.'

'Order anything you need.' Broughton eased the car through a gateway and back on to a rutted farm track. 'I hope your wife will like the cottage. The builders have orders to start work on it as soon as possible. You'll have a Land Rover, too.'

'Hey, look at that fox!' Shank leaned forward, an expression of amazement on his face. Directly in front of them a fox had emerged from the hedgerow and stood its ground in front of the oncoming car. No trace of fear, its arrogance bordered on defiance as it turned to face them. 'God, I wish we'd got a gun with us!'

'The cheeky bugger!' John Broughton's foot slammed down on the accelerator and the Subaru shot forward, suddenly became a four-wheeled missile of death. 'Hold tight!'

The slavering vulpine jaws were wide, the gimlet eyes ablaze with hate, as the suicidal predator tensed as though it was about to hurl itself into battle against all odds. Animal madness, a craziness that defied Nature, Shank thought, feeling cold sweat on his brow. So out of character, a creature that fled from man was now bent on attack against all odds. Any second...

Just when it seemed that the hurtling car must surely run down the fox which stood in its path, the creature twisted to one side, leaped to the safety of the grass verge and disappeared into the undergrowth. Broughton slowed and looked back, but the track behind them was empty.

'Almost!' he laughed. 'I thought we'd got him.'

'There was something strange about that fox,' the gamekeeper muttered. 'Cunning, daring, Reynard is renowned for it, and at times he'll do some funny things, but for a moment I thought that... no, it's crazy.'

'What did you think, then?'

'I thought' – it sounded foolish now that the vulpine had fled – 'that the blighter was going to... to *attack* us!'

'I suppose the foxes have had it their own way too long.' It didn't sound convincing, as if the landowner had to voice a logical reason for the fox's behaviour in order to put both their minds at ease. 'There's been no hunting or shooting over these lands in living memory, so the animals here have learned not to fear man. But all that's going to change from now on. Rig yourself up a vermin gibbet in the woods, Gordon. Hang the bastards up for the rest to see so that they know who's boss.'

The two men lapsed into an uneasy silence. And for some reason John Broughton's thoughts returned to that day months ago when Sir Thomas Corby had finally capitulated and signed away the sanctuary rights of the Corby estate. Like a grim-faced judge unwillingly pronouncing a death sentence. Because he had no choice.

And within the hour Corby himself had died. For no logical reason, he began to worry about Pamela. She was scared; he could tell that the moment he arrived home, in the few minutes he had with her before Gordon Shank arrived, from her black-ringed eyes that denoted a sleepless night, and the way she glanced nervously about her. It was as if her entire personality had changed during the twenty-four hours in which he had been away.

'You sure you're okay?' he had asked, scrutinizing her carefully, noting the way she twisted her fingers nervously together, twining and untwining them.

'I'm okay.' She had averted her gaze. 'Just that I'm not used to being left alone. Not in the country, anyway.'

'Well, I'll be here for a few days,' he reassured her, 'and then some of the new resident staff will be moving in.'

'John, I'm going to . . . to get a dog!'

Christ, now I've heard it all, he thought. Pamela with a bloody dog! She doesn't even *like* animals! 'I'm having a Labrador, darling. A fully trained one from the best kennels in the country. I'm promised it for the start of the shooting season.'

'No, I want one of my own, John!' Her determination bordered on obsession.

'Fine. Go ahead, have a pack of them if you want.'

She nodded and turned away. Then he heard the gamekeeper's van drive up. If Pamela was getting herself a dog then she really was in a bad way.

It was a worrying thought.

3

'A bloody *poodle*!' John Broughton stared aghast at the neatly trimmed dog which yapped playfully and came down the hallway towards him. It jumped up friskily. His inclination was to kick it away, but he refrained and took a deep breath.

'And what is wrong with a poodle?' Pamela stood at the foot of the wide oak staircase, defiance in her expression. 'Aren't I allowed to have a dog of my own? Or do I have to ask permission of the lord of the manor and request a specific breed?'

'No, no, nothing's wrong.' It was rare for John to be taken by surprise. 'I'm just . . . surprised, that's all.'

'You're disapproval is only too evident.' She walked slowly, haughtily, down the hallway. 'Peach, come here, there's a good girl.'

And bloody Peach to boot, he sighed. The dog would not obey. Pamela had to grab it by its collar. She lifted it up into her arms and cradled as she would have done the child which she was unable to bear.

'Don't let him run loose in the woods, though.' It was the instinctive reaction of a shooting man to a dog which did not meet with his approval.

'Because your hired gunman will shoot it if it disturbs his game?' Her eyes blazed angrily. 'Damn you and your pheasants, John. If I'm going to live here, then I'm going to lead a *normal* life. But I won't let *her* near your precious woodlands. That's the last place either of us will go, with snares set all over the place.'

'All right, all right.' He curbed his anger. 'You're free to do as you wish, Pamela. I only said that for the wellbeing of your dog. There's plenty of kennelling space available in the yard. Your poodle won't trouble me, just so long as *I* don't have to feed it and take it walkies!'

'You won't have to do that,' she snapped. 'And Peach isn't going to sleep in a *kennel*, so you can get that idea out of your head. She will sleep at the foot of the bed. And just to show how little you know about dogs, poodles used to be used for retrieving many years ago.' Mrs Beaumont, the woman at the kennels who had sold her the dog, had told her that. Pamela had stored up that bit of seemingly useless information; she knew it would come in handy before long.

John made for the stairs. The sooner this conversation came to a conclusion the better. He wasn't going to win this issue, so he had to learn to live with it. A bloody poodle! What next?

Pamela had decided to take Peach for a walk. The morning was fine and sunny but rain was forecast for later in the day. So she would make the most of the next couple of hours. She would walk across the fields, keep well clear of the home covert, and pay another visit to Jill Shank, the new gamekeeper's wife.

Pamela had spent a couple of hours with her the day before yesterday. Strange, she thought, I wouldn't *dream* of socializing with a working-class girl back in London, but here it is somehow different. A kind of rural classlessness, companionship when you were miles from anywhere and needed somebody to chat to. Not that they had much in common, except that both had a husband whose whole life was devoted to shooting. Jill accepted it, gave Gordon all the support he needed. Maybe, Pamela felt, she had a lot to learn in that respect. Jill was friendly, good fun, told many a country tale in the way it should be told, and had her in fits of laughter. A kind of therapy. Not that they were going to be bosom pals and live in each other's pockets, Pamela reminded herself, but at least they could enjoy a companionship between the lady of the manor and the gamekeeper's wife.

The Shank children were somewhat unruly, Pamela thought. Gary, just fourteen, thought of nothing other than accompanying his father on his rounds, checking those awful fox snares and traps, shooting at what they termed 'vermin'. School was accepted as a necessary evil by the whole family, but they thought no further than rearing pheasants for wealthy gentlemen to shoot. A typical peasant attitude. Gary even had his own gun, bought for his last birthday. Academically, he was probably a dead loss. And the girl, Claire, eleven in May, would sooner go and scatter corn for the few poultry they let run loose round the cottage than behave the way most eleven-year-olds did when they progressed from the doll's-pram stage. The Shanks were content with their lot in life, and in a strange way Pamela Broughton envied them. They didn't have to worry about keeping up with anybody else.

She would walk down to the cottage, stop for a coffee and be back just before one. Not that she would make a routine of these visits, and certainly she wasn't going to have Jill trooping up to the big house with those children, but the occasional visit was a good thing for her husband's sake, and made the gamekeeper feel that he wasn't just a servant. Which he was, of course.

Pamela was aware of the freshness of early spring, a kind of earthy aroma as if the land around had just awakened from its winter hibernation. She heard the drone of a tractor ploughing, rooks cawing noisily over the big wood (and she wasn't going anywhere near there) and woodpigeons cooing in the trees which were just starting to come into bud. There were snowdrops and daffodils in the grass, which soon would be mown and resemble a lawn. Damn it, those rhododendrons ought to be cut down, at the very least cut back, but her husband would not hear of it. He was so insistent that they remained untouched that she had let the matter drop. For now. But she had chalked up a few points for herself over the poodle. All square and ready for the next round.

Peach bounded on ahead, stopping to sniff at strange smells, and looked back when she called. She dangled the leash, a kind of half-threat, but it seemed a shame to have to walk the dog on a lead out here, so far from the main road. After all, it was their own land and half of it was hers, so she could do what she liked in her half. She smiled at the thought. And good for Peach if she does chase the pheasants.

'Don't get *too* far ahead, darling. There's a good girl.' Blast the dog. She was deliberately playing her up; canine fun. But the poodle would have to have some sort of obedience training in a month or two. Perhaps there were doggy classes somewhere in the area. There you go, getting yourself involved in something you swore not to, she scolded herself. 'No, don't go through that hedge, Peachy!'

But Peach was determined to find out what lay on the other side of the dense hawthorn hedge. Impervious to thorns, the dog pushed into the stools, found a gap and went through it. *And seconds later yelped in pain and terror.*

'Oh, my God! Peach, whatever is it?' Pamela panicked and ran forward. Something was surely attacking the poodle — those crazed squeals, and there was a threshing in the hedge. 'I'm coming!'

At first Pamela could not see anything; the hedge was old and thick, and dense even without its summer foliage. Oblivious of the thorns which spiked her and the mud which soaked through her trousers, she knelt down and parted the spiky branches. And gasped in horror when she caught sight of the dog.

The poodle was trapped. A length of stout wire encircled her tiny neck, the other end attached to a heavy chain secured by a stout wooden peg driven into the ground. Peach had ceased struggling, and stood there as if she was on a leash, whimpering pitifully.

'Oh, my poor darling, whatever – ' Realization brought anger. 'It's one of those blasted snares set for a fox!'

Pamela was trembling. The noose was tight around the dog but it did not seem to have harmed Peach in any visible way. She was just caught, unable to escape. How barbaric!

'Keep still, my lovely, and Mummy will soon get you out of that", Pamela's slender fingers stretched out. The dog growled, snarled. She drew her hand away. 'Come on, Peachy, you know I won't hurt you.'

But Peach did not know that. All she understood was that she was trapped and she wasn't going to let anybody touch her. Pamela tried again, and was just quick enough to avoid the small snapping teeth. 'Oh, Peach, how could you?' But the poodle was frightened; her instinct was to bite. Anybody. Pamela pondered. 'Well, this is one of Mr Shank's snares. It's his fault you're caught, so *he* will have to free you. Now, Peach, you'll have to stay there on your own for a few minutes whilst I run and get help. Do you understand?'

Peach did not understand. The moment her mistress was out of sight, the poodle began to struggle again, barking, yelping, whimpering.

Pamela knew that her only hope lay in fetching the gamekeeper. Apart from the fact that it was *his* fault, he would probably have some stout gloves and a pair of wire-cutters; it would take him a matter of seconds to free the dog. She tried to close her ears to the yelping that followed her down the track, and broke into a run. It was a good quarter of an hour from here to the keeper's cottage and, provided Gordon was at home, the same time to get back here. No, they would probably use the Land Rover. Twenty minutes, then, for Peach to endure the trauma of her predicament.

It seemed ages before the slate roof of the cottage came into view, a somewhat dilapidated stone-built structure standing amid a circle of tall Scots pines. There was washing on the line, and Pamela could see Claire in the garden. *Run!*

'Pamela!' Jill Shank had made the initial mistake of calling her 'Pam' on their last meeting and had been politely told it was always 'Pamela'. The keeper's wife stared in amazement, knowing something was wrong. 'Whatever is it?'

'Peach ... my poodle ... caught in a ... bloody snare!'

'Oh!' She was relieved, knowing dogs often got themselves caught in snares and, provided they stood still, came to no harm. 'Don't worry, Gordon's out the back, I'll give him a shout.'

'Oh, it'll be that wire down by the Dingle track,' Gordon Shank smiled. Pamela resisted the urge to slap his face. 'No harm done, Mrs Broughton. It isn't on a bank, so he can't slip and hang himself. Hang on, I'll get the Land Rover and a pair of snippers, and we'll go and get him out.'

'Thank you.' She was pale and shaken. And it's a 'her' not a 'him', and I shouldn't be thanking you, she thought, I should be tearing a strip off you, you bastard. The sooner snares are banned, the better. But she remained silent. Peach's safety was paramount.

Pamela had never been in a Land Rover before. But for her concern for the poodle, she might have refused the offer of a lift and walked. It was filthy inside, mud and straw on the floor, a heap of junk in the back; and, to add insult to injury, there was a bunch of what were obviously those terrible fox-snares hanging from a stanchion, their chains clinking in time with the bumping of the wheels. An upright exhaust belched thick poisonous fumes, the seat was damp and the dirty windscreen obscured her vision. In any other situation she would surely have been carsick. But all she could think of was Peach. Oh, the poor darling must be absolutely terrified by now, she would believe that she had been deserted and left to die. Hurry, oh, *please*, hurry!

Gordon was talking but Pamela wasn't listening. She felt sick, not carsick but just wanting to throw up. But that wouldn't help the poodle. And after we've got her out I'm going to keep her on the leash whenever I take her out, she vowed. And I'll have something to say to John about this! If they must set those snares, then keep them in the woods.

'This is the place.' Gordon was slowing down, the engine missed and almost cut out.

'How do you know?' This long line of hawthorn looked the same to her, she could not be sure.

'See?' He pointed.

'What?' It was difficult to see anything at all through the dirt-smeared glass. She found the catch and eased the door open, then slid out. *Hurry*!

'That piece of string.' She saw where a length of red plastic string dangled from a thorny branch. 'Always mark your wires so you can find 'em again. Count 'em out and count 'em when you take them up so that you don't overlook one. That's the rules.'

She wasn't listening, not to her companion, anyway. Her ears were straining to catch that desperate yelping of the trapped poodle. But there was nothing to be heard except the distant cawing of rooks. 'I think we've come to the wrong place.'

'No, we haven't. There isn't another snare set along here, just the one where I saw that a fox had been crossing. This is the place, all right. Stop there and I'll have your pooch out in a jiffy.'

He reached in the back of the Land Rover and withdrew a pair of very battered secateurs. She saw that he

43

wasn't wearing gloves. Serves you damned well right if Peach bites you, she thought. Then he was on his hands and knees crawling into the prickly hedge bottom.

'Peach isn't barking.' She spoke her fears aloud.

'He's probably got tired and lain down. They usually do.' Gordon Shank turned back, smiling reassuringly.

No, there's something terribly wrong. She was distraught, starting to panic again. She's hanged herself, I know it. Oh, please God, I can't bear it if anything's happened to her. She closed her eyes, didn't want to hear the worst.

'Fucking hell!'

Pamela Broughton winced, not because of the gamekeeper's profanity but because of his tone of shocked horror. She felt utter despair and almost screamed. She heaved and nearly threw up. The very worst *had* happened.

'I'm sorry, Mrs Broughton.' Gordon was out of the hedge, looking up at her, and his lower lip trembled as he spoke. His usually bronzed face was deathly white and the hand holding the wire-cutters shook. 'There's been a . . .'

'Peach is dead, isn't she?' she whispered, recoiling, holding on to the battered Land Rover wing for support. I knew it all along, she realized. I should have let her bite me, anything to save her. Now it's too late.

'I'm afraid she is!'

'They ought to ban those snares. If you must kill foxes, then shoot them, kill them *humanely*. It's awful, leaving them to strangle themselves to death.'

'*The snare didn't kill your poodle, Mrs Broughton!*'

'Oh, my God! What killed her then?'

He did not reply. He stared down at the ground and shook his head.

'What has happened to my dog?'

He was still shaking his head as though in disbelief at what he had just seen in the hedgerow.

'Let me see!' Angry, with a grim determination even

in the face of tragedy and heartbreak, she stepped past him, clawing at the obstructing branches, not caring that they gouged her tender skin. *I want to see for myself!*

She had prepared herself for the sight of the poodle tangled up in that killer wire, eyes bulging, tongue lolling, bleeding where the small teeth had bitten through it. But not for *that!*

The dog was scarcely recognisable as a poodle, or any other miniature species, for that matter. The wire still encircled what was left of its ragged open neck, the bloody throat torn open, the fur matted with blood and mud. The ground was churned up as though some terrible bestial conflict had taken place. One of Peach's legs was almost severed and hung by a sinew. There was a huge open wound in its side and an eye was gone. That was when Pamela Broughton finally vomited.

She was aware of Gordon's strong hands helping her back on to the track. Her vision was blurred. Shock first, she would weep later. *But she had to know what had killed her dog.*

'Oh, God!' she groaned, leaned up against him. 'It's awful. Something killed her. One of your foxes, I suppose.' Like that fox that had bayed her in the moonlight, an evil nocturnal creature, full of hate and viciousness. A vulpine killer.

'No,' he said, 'that was no fox. Not in a million years!'

'What, then? Another dog? Some awful vicious stray found my Peach trapped and helpless?'

'Not a dog, either, Mrs Broughton.' His eyes were narrowed and she was aware of the hand that held her trembling. 'I can hardly believe it, it goes against all the laws of Nature, but I've been in keepering long enough to be able to identify a kill when I see one. The animal which killed your poodle was a *badger!*'

'A badger?' One creature of the wild was much the same as another to her. Why was Shank so shaken because it was a badger and not a fox or a dog? Did it matter? Peach was dead, whatever had killed her it made no difference.

'Badgers *never* attack unless they're cornered, Mrs Broughton. They will maul a terrier below ground in their sett but they'll run a mile if they scent a dog above ground. I just can't believe it, it goes against everything I know. It's . . . weird!'

Gordon Shank felt cold trickles up and down his spine and saw again that fox which had stood its ground and almost attacked the car the day John Broughton was showing him round.

For some uncanny reason, the wild creatures on the Corby estate were not acting naturally. And suddenly it was very frightening.

'I think I'd better take you home.' He helped her back into the Land Rover because for some inexplicable reason he was not happy to let he walk back to Corby House. The spring countryside was no longer peaceful. He sensed an atmosphere of sudden death that transcended a mere animal killing. There was evil in the air.

4

Lucy Titley had walked the Corby lands all her life. Over seventy years ago her mother had pushed her in her pram along this same rutted track that led down past the old woodcutter's cottage to the home covert; she remembered Sir Jasper Corby, Sir Thomas's father, and Lady Corby, who had once invited her up to the big house for afternoon tea. Those were the days! She sighed regretfully in the warm summer sunshine and paused by the stile to gaze across the sloping meadow, a polka-dot landscape of bright yellow buttercups that ran down to the small river. If she stood here and allowed herself to daydream, she could almost convince herself that nothing had changed. Almost, but not quite.

Lucy was tall and straight, with iron-grey hair fastened up in a bun behind her head. Sharp-featured, her expression was one of perpetual discontent as she struggled to right a world that was far from perfect. Bad-tempered where humans were concerned, she was kindly towards animals for her entire life had been devoted, in a strange, obsessional way, towards their wellbeing. Because people simply did not care about animals. Farmers were quite content to turn their sheep and cattle into a field that had no cover other than a hedgerow and leave them there, unfed and at the mercy of the elements. She had once reported the late Sir Jasper to the RSPCA for such an act of cruelty, but nothing had been done about it in spite of her continual reminders to the animal welfare society. Money talked; there was no other explanation. Sir Thomas was as bad as his father. He left the tenant farmers to their business and jetted off abroad somewhere, sunning himself in some tropical climate whilst the Corby livestock struggled to exist in winter conditions. But he had never deliberately inflicted cruelty upon dumb creatures; at least that could be said in his favour. Which was more than one could say for this new landowner, whoever he was.

It was *law* that no animal could be deliberately slaughtered on the estate. *Law*. Decreed two hundred years ago and respected since then. Until now. It was another sign that money was the deciding factor, the criterion, in this modern world. Lucy had contacted the police and asked them if they were aware that birds were being reared here especially to be blasted to death by a team of shooters. The police said there was nothing wrong in that, shooting was perfectly legal provided that those concerned held the necessary shotgun certificates. So she had written to her MP; she had received a reply, eventually, to the effect that it was everybody's *right* to carry a gun and shoot on land where they were entitled to. It was only some time afterwards that she had discovered that Cecil Garrett, MP, was also one of the gun lobby and tarred with the same brush as this fellow Broughton and his cronies. It was all a big cover-up, she raged silently in her small neat cottage on the outskirts of the village. Backhanders from those who could afford them to get what they wanted and flout the law.

So she had written to the antibloodsport people, and at least they were prepared to do something if you read between the lines in their answering letter: '... rest assured that we shall take whatever action is deemed necessary to protect the endangered birds during the coming shooting season'. Which meant demonstrations; Lucy hoped that they would be peaceful ones, but if the lives of pheasants were saved, then the end justified the means. She narrowed her eyes and stared into the distance at the slate roof of the former woodcutter's cottage jutting up over the brow of the field. Her lips tightened. Another cause for anger. For centuries that cottage had been the home of the estate woodcutter, now it housed a gamekeeper. A gamekeeper! They had no right to inflict this upon a land which had been a sanctuary for all dumb creatures for centuries. She would like to set fire to that hovel, raze it to the ground. If she were twenty years younger, more agile, she would.

A movement along the hedgeside attracted her attention. A pair of pointed ears showed above the hawthorn foliage, and then the deafening braying made her jump even though she half-anticipated it. The noise echoed as far as the big wood.

'At least this new fellow has kept Major on.' She spoke aloud as an ageing dark brown donkey came into view, stuck its head through a gap in the hedge and eyed her hopefully. Damn it, she should have remembered to bring some Polos for Major; it was an unforgivable oversight on her part. 'I'm terribly sorry, old chap, I forgot.' She stroked his nose warily because he sometimes gave a playful nip. 'I'm going to keep a strict eye on you, Major,' she promised, 'and at the first sign of neglect I'm going to telephone the donkey sanctuary and have you taken into care. You can't trust these people; if they derive enjoyment from slaughtering birds, there's no knowing what they might decide to do to a donkey!' She recalled having read a couple of years or so ago how the people from the donkey sanctuary had gone to the rescue of a donkey in Spain, a poor old fellow just like Major which the villagers were going to kill in a sick ritual. She wouldn't put it past these bloodsport villains to try something like that! 'I'll be keeping a very strict eye on you. And that reminds me, I'd better just check that your feet are being trimmed. If they're not . . .'

Lucy had to walk back to the stile, the donkey keeping pace with her on the other side of the thick hedge. He brayed again. Somehow it sounded different. Almost . . . *angry*. If he's upset, she concluded, it's because of *them*. Ah, that's better, I can see now. Leaning forward, bending over the stile, she studied those animal hooves in the grass. They had not been trimmed. Major seemed to be rocking back on his feet, unable to stand firmly, in a posture of discomfort. Lucy's eyes narrowed. 'I shall warn them, first.' Her cheeks were flushed. 'Just one warning, and if they haven't attended to you by this time tomorrow . . .'

She gave a cry of pain and almost sprawled forward over the rickety stile in a moment of dizziness. She was aware of something warm and sticky trickling down the side of her face and instinctively pulled away from the donkey, wrenching her ear free of the animal's teeth.

'*Major*!' She checked her anger and fingered her bleeding ear. Just a nip. The skin was broken, nothing worse. But it wasn't the donkey's fault. He was normally so docile, and if he was becoming bad-tempered then it was either because of his advancing years or because of *them* – more likely the latter, she concluded. Still rubbing her ear, she stared at the creature. Its head was thrust forward in an almost aggressive pose, his lips were drawn back in what could only be interpreted as a snarl. Lucy was shocked and hurt. 'Major! After all the sweeties I've brought you, and we've known each other for twelve years, then you go and do a thing like that! I'm ashamed of you.' She held out her hand in a gesture of peace, at the same time stepping back a couple of paces so that the donkey was unable to reach her. She wondered with some trepidation if Major was able to leap the stile. She did not know whether donkeys could jump or not. It was a disconcerting thought.

He gave another loud bray, which reminded Lucy of one of those caged lions that time her mother had taken her to the zoo, a frustrated and angry beast roaring its wrath against mankind. It wasn't its fault. She felt sorry for the animal. Pity and . . . fear! Lucy stepped back another pace. Major was scraping the ground with an untrimmed hoof, flicking his tail from side to side, glaring malevolently at her. That hurt her far more than the pain from her bitten ear. Poor Major, it wasn't his fault; maltreatment had made him this way. She would go down to the cottage and confront that gamekeeper fellow. The donkey was his responsibility. Whatever you've been doing to Major, you haven't been looking after his feet, she'd tell him. Has he been wormed, had his booster injections? Where's his salt-lick? And I hope for your sake, my man, that you give him some shelter at night! I want all these matters attended to right away, and I shall be back first thing in the morning. If I'm not satisfied then I'm telephoning the donkey sanctuary and the RSPCA.

Another ear-shattering bray from the donkey; he was pushing at the stile now, the fragile rustic frame threatening to collapse under his weight. Lucy turned and began to walk as fast as she could in the direction of the distant cottage. A discreet glance back over her shoulder showed that the stile had not collapsed... yet! The donkey was snorting, clearly angry. Don't run, don't let him see you're frightened, she told herself. It wasn't easy.

Now she heard Major on the other side of the hedge, keeping pace with her. She tried to recall if there were any places further along where he might squeeze through; she could not think of any. The donkey brayed its anger again at being thwarted. And then Lucy Titley saw the snake in the track ahead of her.

She knew it was an adder. She had lived in the countryside long enough to be able to differentiate between the only two British species of snakes, adders and grass snakes. The viper was about two feet long, its flat head raised off the ground, its coppery-coloured eyes fixed unwaveringly on her. Outstretched, obviously in the act of crossing the track from one clump of undergrowth to another, its reddish-brown body had those unmistakable dark arrow-like markings on it. Lucy halted and watched it.

She was not afraid, just wary. She knew that although the venom of this species was poisonous (she remembered some years ago a bilberry-picker in the park receiving a nasty bite) these snakes were shy, preferring to slither away at the approach of humans, and only attacked if they were accidentally trodden upon. This one was obviously curious. Perhaps it had never encountered a human being before. Any second, it would scuttle on its way. She waited; behind the hedge she could hear Major scraping angrily at the dry ground again. She hoped the adder wouldn't bite him.

The snake made no move to continue on its journey, just remained where it was, watching her. Its eyes glinted in the sunlight. Red and ... *evil*. She shuddered. Now you're being silly, Lucy Titley, she thought. That adder will no more harm you than it will sprout wings and fly...

The snake moved so fast that she had no warning of its intentions. It flung itself forward and was upon her before she had a chance to flee, throwing itself at her. She screamed and staggered back. It was like a needle gouging into her exposed ankle above her flat shoe. Excruciating pain! The adder flicked from side to side, hissing. In revulsion and fear, through a scarlet haze, she saw it come free of her, turn and disappear into the long grass. *Oh, God, it's bitten me!*

In sheer terror she panicked, limping away on her already swelling leg, aware that the donkey was braying again. I need help, at once, she realized. I might die! Ten yards down the track she stopped, suddenly remembering that it was over a mile back to the village. She felt faint and wanted to be sick. Instinctively, she threw up. She would never make it, she despaired. They would find her lying here, dead! How long did it take to die from a viper's bite? She had no idea. She glanced down at her injured foot, turning away as she saw the ugly swelling. It was full of pus, poison. It would travel through her system; already it might be too late.

And then she remembered the cottage. It could not be more than three hundred yards away, and this track led down to it. She had been on her way there, and it was her only hope. Her gait was ungainly, and she resisted the desire to rest because once she stopped she might not get going again. Her vision was blurred, with a kind of autumnal mist streaked with red before her eyes. Major followed her – only the hedge separating them – giving voice angrily every so often, almost a note of triumph in his tone as though he was rejoicing at her misfortune. That was stupid, she thought, her imagination running riot. *I just... have to... keep going.*

The cottage loomed up ahead of her, its stone structure almost hidden by steel scaffolding, a bonfire smouldering in the untended garden. Rubble littered the ground, strewn everywhere. She tried to shout but all she managed was a whisper. Suppose there was nobody at home! In which case there was no hope for her because she had not the strength to make it all the way back to the main road.

A woman appeared in the open doorway. Thank God! Lucy clung feebly to the remnants of a rotted garden gate and saw the woman running towards her, a young girl following her and saying, 'Mummy, that lady looks ill.'

'Whatever's the matter?' Jill Shank caught Lucy's outstretched hand, and in the same instant saw the huge swelling. 'Oh, Lord, you've been bitten by an adder!'

'Not the . . . snake's fault,' Lucy muttered as she allowed herself to be led indoors and seated on a frayed sofa in the untidy kitchen, even in the midst of her pain wrinkling her nose in disgust at the overpowering stench of stale cooking.

'My husband's not here.' Jill was trembling. 'So I'd best ring the hospital. Just you sit there quiet. Claire' – motioning to the young girl – 'pour the lady a cup of tea and put plenty of sugar in it. Hurry!'

Lucy sipped the strong tea, aware of the woman talking in the hallway, then heard her coming back into the room.

'The snake,' Jill's voice trembled. 'The hospital want to know if you killed it.'

'Killed it!' Lucy sat upright, indignant and angry. 'I wouldn't kill a snake, no matter what. How dare they suggest such a thing!'

Jill was back from the phone again, bustling. 'I've got to take you right in. Now. They hoped you'd killed the snake. Apparently they can tell from it how much serum you need. But you haven't, and that's that. Now, hold on to me and I'll help you outside. It's lucky Gordon didn't take the Land Rover.'

'It's crazy,' Gordon Shank picked at his overcooked rabbit stew and shook his head in disbelief. 'A bloody adder *attacking* a human!'

'I thought adder bites were fairly common,' Jill answered from the sink. 'You remember that youth got bitten when we were at Manley. And that farmworker at – '

'Yes, but both of them *trod* on the bloody snakes!' He snapped irritably. 'Adders will only bite if you step on them or molest them. According to this woman, it was crossing the path and it *attacked* her. Which isn't natural, they just don't do that. No more than badgers attack a dog even if it is caught in a snare. That's what's worrying me. This whole place is creepy.' He shuddered. 'Something else . . . I went up to the spinney this morning, the one they call Spion Kop, to give those bloody rooks a pasting. I shot one, the rest kept their distance, circling high and cawing. But I got the feeling . . . it sounds crazy' – he paused – '*that if I hadn't had the gun, the whole bloody flock would have swooped down and attacked me!*'

5

Gary Shank liked weekends, next best thing to the school holidays, because then he could become a gamekeeper for real. He thought that school was a waste of time, and he knew that secretly his parents thought so too, because he wasn't taught anything about gamekeeping. He needed to be able to read and write, add up a few figures, but apart from that schooling was irrelevant to his chosen career. Another year and he would be helping Dad full time. Even before then he would have a full fortnight of term time on the work opportunity scheme.

After he left school, Dad said, they would dispense with John, the part-time helper, and Gary could replace him. Roll on the next twelve months!

His father allowed him to operate his own network of tunnel traps and fox snares throughout the year. This meant getting up early and going his rounds before school, but he didn't mind that. Last week he had caught two foxes and shot them both with his single-barrel twenty bore as they pulled at the wire noose which encircled their necks. There had been fourteen grey squirrels in the traps – catching them was a cinch – and three stoats and a weasel. He had baited the rat holes in the river bank, and in between accounted for three magpies and a carrion crow with his gun. He had his own vermin gibbet in the spinney beyond the home covert and he was proudly keeping count of the rotting corpses strung up there. He wanted Mr Broughton to see them, proof of his keepering skills and surely a passport to a full-time job on the estate after his schooling was finished.

And today was Saturday, which meant two whole days doing what he loved most of all in life. No lie-in for Gary, he was up just after six to remove another three squirrels from the traps. Then it was back home for a quick breakfast and time to go and feed the pheasant poults in the release pen. His father was letting him do that on his own now, and proudly he carried a bucket of pheasant food in one hand, his gun in the other. He never went anywhere without his gun; a keeper should carry one at all times – you never knew when the opportunity to account for a vermin species might present itself.

The release pen occupied a full acre of the big wood. It consisted of eight-foot-high wire mesh buried six inches in the ground, tapering funnels at intervals so that the birds could go out into the wood and return to roost at night, and just one entrance door. The whole pen was circuited by an electric fence to keep the marauding foxes at bay. Trees and undergrowth grew inside the compound, ample vegetation for the birds to shelter beneath on wet days. As the poults grew and foraged further afield, the more they needed feeding to encourage them to return to the pen, to regard it as their home. There were five hundred pheasants in this one, smaller numbers in the other pens situated in the adjoining woods. There was going to be some sport for the guns this coming season, for sure!

Gary knew that his father and mother were worried. Certainly the creatures of the wild had been acting strangely these past weeks. First there had been that business of a badger killing Mrs Broughton's poodle, then Miss Titley had been bitten by a snake. She had recovered, after spending a few days in hospital, and was back making a nuisance of herself on the Corby estate. She had reported Dad to the RSPCA for neglecting the donkey's feet; the hooves had been trimmed, and now everybody was satisfied. Apart from Miss Titley. The silly old cow had been nosing in the wood, trying to open the door of the pen to let the pheasants out, only the padlock and chain had thwarted her efforts. She had not even tried to do it surreptitiously; she had been waiting there when Gary and his father came with the evening feed and had *demanded* that the birds were given their freedom. Gordon had told her to bugger off, and eventually she had gone. But she would be back, the boy reflected, and it would serve her bloody well right if she got another adder bite. All the same, his father said that they had to be on their guard, against both the old spinster and the creatures of the woods.

A strange thing had happened only yesterday morning. Gary furrowed his brow as the memory of it returned. One of his traps, the one down by the footbridge over the river, had killed a stoat. As he approached, another stoat appeared out of the undergrowth and stood its ground aggressively. It seemed as if the small, bloodthirsty animal was about to attack, tensing itself as if to spring at him; usually it would have fled at his advance. Whether or not it would actually have launched itself at him, he would never know, because he brought up his gun swiftly and fired, virtually cutting the carnivore in two at a distance of no more than five yards. Another case of unnatural animal behaviour. The boy kept a cartridge in his gun now, even though his father had told him not to load it unless he was expecting a shot. On the Corby estate you were always expecting a shot these days.

Some rooks flew up out of the unroofed release pen at Gary's approach, calling angrily and noisily at having been disturbed from their feed of scattered corn. A couple settled in the topmost branches of a leafy oak. He could just see them amidst the foliage. He put down the bucket and was in the act of mounting his gun when he checked his impulse; he couldn't shoot here, the noise would frighten the pheasants. One of the corvines cawed, an arrogant jibe as though it *knew* it was safe. Hell, it should have flown off with the others, but it just sat up there watching him put his gun down and fumble for the padlock key. Cheeky bastard, he thought, as soon as I've gone it'll drop down to continue its feed of expensive corn!

He unlocked the gate and squeezed inside, leaving his gun outside propped up against a tree. He heard the rustling of pheasants in the bushes. The place was alive with them – as it should be. He glanced at the big hopper situated in an open clearing, a twenty gallon oil drum with holes drilled in the bottom so that the corn could filter out. It would need topping up tomorrow, he noticed, but you had to hand-feed as well, let the birds get to know you and come to your whistle. Gary whistled.

The undergrowth moved. Pheasants began to show themselves, dozens of scrawny hens with bare patches on their bodies where they had been feather-pecked. Some were bleeding. Cruel buggers! A cock pheasant, bigger than the rest, a melanistic with dark plumage, eyed the young gamekeeper, watched him. Gary shivered, that bird was evil, a nasty one, bigger than the rest, a bully who was probably responsible for much of the feather-pecking. *I'd like to wring your bloody neck,* he thought.

Gary scattered a couple of handfuls of corn on the ground. The waiting birds came closer but they did not immediately start to peck at the grain as they normally did. Two, three, dozen, more came out of the undergrowth. *Just watching him.*

He backed away a step, licking his lips. His mouth was dry. *What the hell's the matter with you lot?* They were bunching, still more birds arriving. A carpet of them, all eyeing him, the big cock in the foreground.

He tossed some more corn, throwing it so that it fell amongst his feathered audience, hit them, and bounced off like a golden hailstorm. They did not even appear to notice, too busy watching the boy, a myriad of tiny eyes glittering in a shaft of sunlight which beamed down through a canopy of overhead leaves. Gary shifted his position uneasily. There was definitely something wrong here.

The cock pheasant strode angrily forward, paused to peck at a fallen grain, then threw it to one side. A gesture of contempt: *We're not interested in corn, boy, just you!*

The big bird was less than a foot away from Gary's feet now. Head erect, it gave a chuckling call, a sort of rallying sound. The beak darted, and thudded against the rubber of the boy's wellington boots. Again and again. Gary kicked out, caught the pheasant and knocked it away, but it came back again. Fearless. Angry.

'Fuck off, you!' And I don't care if my mother does hear me, he thought. 'Go on, *shoo!*'

Now other pheasants were moving in, a hustling mass of them, all around his feet, beaks stabbing, unable to penetrate the rubber, but he could feel them through it. It was frightening. He kicked them away but there were too many of them, each and every one of them intent on pecking at his boots. It's because my wellies are green, he decided, searching for a logical explanation. They think it's grass, like the poultry sometimes do when you go near them in snowy weather. But it wasn't winter and these pheasants seemed to have an obsession with his footwear. And there was no mistaking their ferocity.

He glanced behind him; the door was only a matter of yards away but there were dozens of them in between him and his only escape route. He fought down his rising panic. Sod 'em, *he* was the gamekeeper here, they were his charges. You didn't get scared of pheasants, you handled thousands of the buggers every year; crated them, transported them from the pens to the woods, wrung the necks of wounded ones on shooting days. You didn't think twice about picking them up. They were stupid birds. Like now.

He tipped the rest of the corn, upended the bucket and showered corn all over the foremost birds, but they seemed oblivious of the deluge of food where as normally they scratched and fought one another for it. Icy fingers stroked his back. 'Go on, get out of my bleedin' way. I've got work to do!'

If anything, more birds came to join the throng, a forest of darting, stabbing beaks. He thought, we should have put 'bits' on them earlier to stop the feather-pecking, that would have stopped this nonsense. Except that it was too late now. He moved, trod on a poult, and felt its leg crack beneath his weight. A surge of angry, sparsely feathered creatures, they flung themselves at his legs, fluttering and scratching with their immature claws; grasping, hissing.

Suddenly there was a flutter of wings and the cock was airborne, hurling itself at Gary. He threw up an arm to defend himself, but was not quite quick enough.

The bird's spurs raked his cheek; only his elbow deflected them from his eye. He yelled in pain, staggered back and nearly fell, then trod on another pheasant. The cock dropped down, strutted haughtily and tensed for another attack. A rush of wings, then something struck Gary on the back, tore at his jacket and became caught up. It was hanging there, scratching at him, pecking. He reached behind him and felt a sharp pain on his hand as he dislodged his attacker. And now his terror was mounting.

Out of the corner of his eye he spied his gun leaning up against a tree outside the pen. Oh, God, if he had only brought it inside with him! But he hadn't; he was defenceless, and these crazed pheasants were massing for an all-out onslaught on him.

A clamour of wings, and he was only just in time to turn his back. He cried out as a rush of birds hit him, scratching and pecking as they fluttered back to the ground. The gate, he had to reach it at all costs; that cock bird was calling, a harsh '*cock-up, cock-up*', urging his harem to a full-scale assault on the human intruder in their domain. Gary ran. There were pheasants all around his feet. He trod on them, staggered, and fell.

Instinctively he rolled himself up into a ball and covered his head with his arms, the way he did at school when the rugby scrum collapsed. They were all over him, scratching, pecking, fluttering, fighting for a glimpse of exposed flesh. He smelled them, the acrid stench of their droppings sharp in his nostrils. He was screaming, and screaming again, because he knew he would never make it to the gate.

Vicious beaks gouged his neck and hands, drawing blood. And the sight of crimson crazed them as it did when they feather-pecked one another. He was just a heap of humanity crawling with birds that suddenly lusted for flesh, grain-eaters that had become carnivores. More cocks joined the fray, uttering cries of hate and bloodlust, determined to kill their victim now that they had him at their mercy. With frenzied birdcalls and scraping claws they tore the boy's clothing because they knew that beneath the flimsy material lay tender flesh that would ribbon and turn scarlet beneath their stabbing beaks.

Gary had given up screaming and was sobbing now, and no longer striking out at the pheasants. One of them had penetrated his jacket and was trying to tear a hole in his shirt. His cap had fallen off and a bird was pecking at his head, each jab going deeper and deeper.

'*What the fuck's going on?*' The voice came from somewhere beyond the scrabbling din of the pheasants. Gary heard it dimly, but dared not raise his head up from the ground to look. Familiar, not his father; he tried to place it but failed. He felt relief that somebody had found him, but what chance did they stand against this army of attacking pheasants?

A metallic clang, that was the outer gate opening. *Oh, please help me*!

'Go on, get back!' Whoever it was obviously thought that his presence would frighten the birds. It wouldn't.

It didn't.

A moment later a booming report ripped through the release pen. Gary felt the birds leave him. There was a sudden rush of wings and the sound of panic-flying pheasants thudding into trees and against the mesh surround of the release pen. Scurrying through the undergrowth, they were fleeing, hiding. Only then did he look up.

It was John Broughton, clad in a checked shirt and cotton trousers, Gary's smoking twenty bore in his hands. Dazed, the boy looked around him; there wasn't a pheasant in sight.

'Are you all right?' Broughton knelt by his side and examined the cuts on his face and neck. 'My God, what happened?'

'I . . . I don't know,' Gary looked round, fearful lest the hand-reared pheasants might be massing for another attack. 'I came in to feed them. Then . . . then they . . . just *attacked* me.'

'We'd best get you home,' Broughton helped him up, and supported him. 'I don't think you're hurt much apart from a few pecks and scratches, but it could have been decidedly nasty. What the devil is going on in this place eh?'

'I've never heard of pheasants attacking people.' There was concern on John Broughton's face. Gary was indoors, having his wounds bathed by his mother. Fortunately, nothing required hospital treatment. 'One thing after another, Gordon. Not just foxes and badgers, but *all* wildlife on the estate.'

'I know.' The gamekeeper's features were pallid beneath his sunburn. 'Even that damned donkey tried to bite Jill when she went down to give it an apple. And if there's a bee in the vicinity you can bet your boots that it'll try to sting you.' He held up his arm, displayed a red swelling that was beginning to go down. 'That bugger had me this morning. You almost find yourself believing what they're saying down in the village.'

'And what's that, Gordon?'

'That the Corby Curse has come true.' The keeper tried to grin but his lower lip trembled. 'They say that two hundred years ago one of the Corby ancestors declared the estate an animal sanctuary for all time, and because that pact with Nature has been broken the wild animals and birds are taking their revenge.'

'Which is absolute bloody poppycock!' Somehow, John Broughton's words lacked conviction. 'Isn't it, Gordon?' He was looking to the gamekeeper for confirmation, support.

'Yes,' he replied lamely. 'It can't be anything like that. Maybe it's the aftermath of Chernobyl.'

'Could be.' But whatever the cause, Broughton

thought, the fact remains that the animals are hellbent on attacking *us*. 'I think we'd better carry guns wherever we go, whatever job we're doing. We can't take any more chances. If in doubt, shoot!'

'I suppose so.'

'But we're not going to let bloody animals get the better of us!' Broughton's jaw jutted, his expression was grim. 'I bought this estate to develop the sporting potential and, by God, I'll do just that! If necessary, Gordon, chuck the pheasant food in through the wire. Don't take any risks with them. Take it from me, when the shooting season opens we'll get our bloody own back on the buggers!' He laughed but it sounded hollow. 'Keep in touch. I must dash, I've an appointment and Pamela will slay me if we're late.'

As he watched the Subaru drive away, Gordon Shank felt the shivers that had been slowly climbing up his spine spread into his scalp. He shuddered in the warm sunshine. It had been close, touch and go. If Broughton had not taken it into his head to go up and look at the poults in the release pen . . . it did not bear thinking about. Another sudden nagging worry: John Simpson, the part-time keeper who helped in the evenings and at weekends, was up on Spion Kop somewhere, feeding the pheasants in the pen there. The youth wasn't carrying a gun, he rarely did . . .

Gordon Shank began walking towards the Land Rover. He had to get up there. Fast.

John Simpson had begun his working life on one of the Corby farms on the Youth Training Scheme. Slightly overweight and permanently dishevelled, his greatest failing was an inherent laziness. His only talent was his ability to shirk hard work. He could always find a reason for being elsewhere when there was a job to be done. And that sunny Saturday morning was no exception.

Mr Whitmore, the home farm manager, would certainly not take him on permanently once the training period had expired. John was not sorry; farm labouring was not his vocation, anyway. But he had thought gamekeeping would be much easier; he had read somewhere that a gamekeeper was 'somebody who walked round with a gun under his arm and did nowt else'. Once again he had been disillusioned. Mr Shank would not allow him to carry a gun, not even his old Daisy air rifle. It wasn't much different from farming – humping sacks of feedstuffs about, attending to fencing. And now he was being ordered to lug this twenty-kilo bag of corn all the way up to that small wood on the top of the hill. Fuck that for a game of soldiers!

The pheasants had a hopper full of grain in the pen, anyway; they didn't need this lot as well. He followed the winding course of the river bank and, once out of sight of the keeper's cottage, he stopped and looked around to make sure there was nobody in sight. There wasn't, just a mallard swimming nonchalently in the shallows with a brood of week-old ducklings.

'Here,' he called softly, 'I've got sommat for you.'

The duck kept her distance, watching him intently. He upended the plastic sack, showering its contents into the water, and watched the grain sinking to the bottom and settling in the mud. 'There you are, then. Please your bleedin' selves whether you eat it or not. But at least I don't 'ave to carry it up the hill!'

He sank down on to his haunches. Shank would not be expecting him back for at least another hour; if he returned earlier, the keeper might be suspicious and would, in all probability, find him another tedious chore. Far better to take it easy here, rest awhile and go back later, he decided. He stretched himself out on the soft grass and closed his eyes. This was the life, this was the gamekeeping job he had dreamed about. And they were bloody well paying him for it!

The sounds of the countryside were all around him, and he murmured his own contented sleepy accompaniment. The duck was quacking, encouraging its brood to dive down and pick the corn off the river bed; grasshoppers were chirping in the long grass; and bees droned as they searched diligently for nectar, a soft soothing noise that made him drowsy. He had plenty of time for a nap, and it would make up for having to get up so early to feed the bloody pheasants. Which hadn't been fed, he sniggered to himself.

He came out of his doze with a sharp cry of pain. Swatting at his face, he felt something crunch beneath his hand. Fucking hell! It was as though somebody had crept up on him whilst he slept and stuck a needle into his cheek. He stared in horror at the squashed insect which adhered to his palm. *A bee*! The fucker had stung him. He moaned as the fleshy pain increased, and rubbed at the wound. But it only hurt all the more. Groaning, he got up on his knees, knowing that he would have to go back and get Mrs Shank to put something on it, some soothing cream; anything that would alleviate the escalating pain. He winced. That bloody noise was louder, more like the sound of the helicopter which had come to spray the fields at the home farm last week than an insect hum. A buzzing that was no longer peaceful, more of an angry whine that grew louder by the second. Louder. And still louder.

The swarm hit John Simpson before he saw them. It came from behind him on the opposite side of the river, a dense cloud of angry wild bees which had singled out their victim and dived straight in to the attack, unerring insect spitfires, landing, stinging, swarming. He screamed. As he opened his mouth one crawled inside and stung him on the tongue. He tried to pull it out, two more entered, lodged on his gum and stung him. The pain was blinding.

Now they were on every inch of exposed flesh, going down inside the open neck of his shirt. Sheer pain and terror drove him one way, then the other. He slipped, and almost fell into the sluggish flowing river. Staggering back on to his feet, agonized, crazed, he stumbled into a blind, heedless flight. He closed his eyes, but the bees stung the lids and jerked them open. They were crawling in his ears, in his hair, falling off as they spent their venom, only to be replaced by others, a back-up force following on, their macabre music like a chainsaw gone berserk. Frenzied, they were driving him before them. Bent double, he clutched at his groin because they had found their way down there, too. His back arched in agony, then he doubled forward again.

Somehow he found his way back on to the main track and just followed it, not knowing whether he was heading towards the keeper's cottage or on course for the main road. He swallowed, and felt a bee slip down his throat; he tried to vomit it back but it stuck. He knew he couldn't carry on much further. Everywhere was starting to go dark. The twilight was streaked with scarlet. The noise was louder, deeper – different somehow, but did it really matter? He couldn't see at all now; his night had fallen. He heard shouting. He thought at first it was his own voice, then he smelled the acrid stench of diesel fumes. The drone was a deeper pitch, almost like an engine ticking over. But he didn't care, he didn't care about anything now.

And suddenly somebody was beating him, slapping him. Blows to the face and body knocked him to his knees; it felt like an assault with one of those fire brooms which were deposited all over the estate, birching him for his laziness, his deceit. He mumbled pleas for mercy and at last the beating stopped. Strong hands clasped him beneath his armpits and began to drag him along the ground, then hoist him up. He knew he was in a vehicle, sprawled in the seat. And a voice which he vaguely recognized as belonging to Gordon Shank and seemed miles away was saying, 'The sooner we get you to hospital, the better, laddie!'

At some stage during the bumpy, uneven journey he felt consciousness finally slipping away from him.

6

Adrian Roberts lay back on the grassy bank and wished that he could have just five minutes of peace and quiet. Five minutes, and he would be quite satisfied. It wasn't much to ask. He glanced apprehensively towards his old Mini van parked on the verge, shabby and rusted, the nearside door primed red in contrast to the hand-painted blue of the rest of the vehicle. If he had stayed at home today he would have been able to put a coat of paint on that, to make it look reasonably respectable. But did it really matter? The MOT was due in September and the van would not pass without a new subframe, and that was something he could not afford. He bemoaned his luck – he was beginning to face up to the realities of life.

Tall and fair-haired, he had enjoyed twenty-seven years of sheltered life in a middle-class home, a public-school education and a promising future in his father's light engineering business. No worries. Until Liza came on the scene. He watched his wife with a smouldering resentment; damn her, she was going to wake the baby up to feed it, and that was surely an end to his hopes of a Sunday afternoon's relaxation! Liza was the root of all his problems. Petite and dark-haired, she would have been very attractive if it hadn't been for that turned-up nose. Once, he had thought it gave her a pertness; now he decided it detracted from the rest of her, reduced her to what she was – a cheeky wench off the council estate at the rear of his parents' home. Class distinction, they had said. And they had been right. He couldn't see it then but he could now. And it was too damned late. She wouldn't rise up to his status, she would drag him down to hers. And the cunning little bitch had deliberately planned it, set out to catch herself a rich man's son so that she could live comfortably for the rest of her life. Only it had backfired on both of them. Now Adrian didn't have a job at his father's office, nor was he likely to inherit that which was rightfully his. Joe Roberts had kicked his son's arse right out of the door, and that was that, unless there was a reconciliation at a later stage. But Adrian's father was the type who didn't forgive or forget.

The baby woke up and stared to cry. Adrian could see Liza sitting in the passenger seat, her blouse undone, trying to force a nipple into the resisting infantile mouth. At three months, Sam had all the traits of his grandfather; he was as stubborn and single-minded as Adrian's father. Screaming now, he was kicking and flaying his arms and legs, bawling his bloody little head off. Adrian closed his eyes. Liza was talking daft to the little bugger, her raucous tones grating on her husband's ears. She was a perpetual complainer, a whiner. And she had kept that hidden until she got what she wanted. Now he was on the dole, and the only home they had was a room in her folks' council semi – and if the council found out, as they surely would before long, then they'd be out in the street.

He sighed. Any second she would be shouting for him to come and help. And what can I do if the little bleeder doesn't want his dinner? he thought. Not a lot. It all created tension that couldn't be left behind even on a summer Sunday afternoon drive into the countryside. There was no hiding place where Adrian's problems were concerned.

Less than a couple of years ago his relationship with Liza had been a very exciting one. His father had disapproved of his son seeing a girl off the estate but had tolerated it; Adrian did not take Liza back to his home. Most evenings he called for her and they went for a drive, dropping in at a pub. And then parked up in some country lane for hours afterwards. Her body excited him, especially when it was unclothed and sprawled seductively in the back seat of his Chevette.

She had been around, she made no secret of the fact, and he had found it erotic. He took precautions and did not foresee any problems. Until that night just before Christmas when they went to a dance in town. It was very mild for the time of year and they stopped off in their usual courting place, a muddy lane with some convenient farm gateway about a mile from home.

He had had too much to drink. If the police had stopped him then he would surely have lost his licence. With hindsight, the law would have done him a favour because then he and Liza would not have ended up in the back seat. He was vulnerable that night and his girlfriend exploited his weakness.

'Ade.' He detested the way she had taken to shortening his name recently. 'I . . . I don't want to . . . to *use* anything tonight!'

'Eh!' A sudden fear, a thrill, had him pulsing in her seductively rubbing fingers. 'God, I might get you pregnant!'

'No.' Her eyes narrowed in the wan glow of the dashboard lights. 'I'm safe at the moment, it'll be all right.'

Temptation. He hesitated, and she stroked him again. He wondered what it would be like without a condom.

'Go on,' she urged, laughing. 'I'd love it.'

He succumbed, and it was all over in a few minutes. Breathtakingly exciting, and then the worry. Six weeks of near panic when, in reply to his daily question, she smiled and said, 'No, but perhaps I'll start tomorrow.'

She hadn't. And tomorrow had never come. Which was why he was here now. Liza had changed, for the worse. Nagging, all she thought about was that damned baby. Adrian had not had a decent night's sleep since it was born, and it was painfully clear that he was about to be denied a doze in the warm sunshine. He didn't like babies; there was no point in trying to be a martyr about it. When Liza was rushed into hospital in the middle of the night, he found himself hoping that it would be stillborn. A terrible thought, but it would let him off the hook. Without a child he would have made the break and sought a reconciliation with his father; his mother might have talked him round. But Sam had been born a healthy eight pounds, and that was that. Adrian went through a spell of forced paternal affection; it was hard work, a deception that petered out into resignation to his fate. If he had had a job it would not have been so bad, at least he would have been away from home for a few hours in the day. As it was, he had that brat squalling day and night, and Liza's mother got on his nerves. The cow seemed to think it was great having him living with them. He couldn't take much more, he was going to have to do *something*.

'E won't take it.' Her complaining voice again. 'I 'ope there's nowt the matter with 'im.'

'He's probably not hungry.' And, like me, he needs his sleep, Adrian thought. 'Put him back to sleep and maybe later he'll feel like it.'

'I suppose so. 'Ere, give me a hand to get the carrycot out of the back.'

Reluctantly he rose to his feet. Maybe Sam would go to sleep for an hour or so, and if Liza would just shut up in the meantime there was a faint possibility that Adrian *might* get forty winks. He wasn't counting on it, just hoping.

'There, ain't 'e just beautiful.' Liza had positioned the carrycot in the middle of the van. Sam had stopped crying and he looked sleepy.

No, Adrian thought, I don't think he's beautiful at all. In fact, I think he's bloody ugly. All babies were ugly, repulsive little things; he could not understand why women got so excited about them. 'He'll sleep now. Why don't we take the opportunity to have a nap as well?'

'It seems a shame to sleep on such a beautiful day.' Apparently today was one of those day when everything was going to be 'beautiful' for Liza. When she was in one of those moods she chattered incessantly, an unending stream of drivel, talking for the sake of it. If she had had a nice voice, or could have conducted an intelligent conversation, he could have understood it. God, her voice grated on him! Dad had been right, he grudgingly admitted to himself.

Adrian lay back on the grassy bank and closed his eyes. One thing was certain, he couldn't stand this much longer.

'I wish we lived in the countryside proper.' As predicted, his wife began to talk. 'Well, you know what I mean, Ade. Away from other 'ouses, just ourselves. You, me and 'im.' He envisaged her jerking a thumb in the direction of their sleeping son. 'It's much 'ealthier in the country, ain't it? You feel you've got room to breathe and you 'aven't got neighbours watchin' you all the time. You know what I mean?'

He grunted. You wouldn't know what to do with yourself if you hadn't got some of your gossipy friends walking into the house as if they lived there every five minutes, he thought. And you wouldn't have a bingo session Wednesdays and Fridays. You'd never survive. Now shaddup!

'I *love* the countryside, Ade. The smell of the fields and the sound of the birds. Know what I mean? And it brings back memories, doesn't it for you?' She gave a laugh.

'Like what?'

'Like parkin' in a gateway and ... well, you know what I'm on about.' Her straying fingers left him in no doubt.

'Uh-huh.'

'Don't get romantic, will you?' Her tone sharpened.

'Sorry.'

'That was a night, wasn't it?'

'Which night?'

'Don't tell me you've forgot already, and with Sam bawlin' and blartin' to remind yer.'

'Oh, yes, of course.' Now she was going to start gloating. 'We'll never 'ave it again quite like that, will we?'

'How d'you mean?'

'Well, you so bloomin' careful all the time and then me actually persuadin' you to leave yer French letter off. Remember?' She was squeezing and rubbing him through his trousers. And, damn it, he was becoming aroused. But there was something he had always wanted to know, and maybe this was the time to get it out of her. Just for the satisfaction of knowing.

'It was exciting,' he agreed, keeping his eyes closed. 'But you said it was all right, that you were safe.'

'Did I?' Mock surprise, a snigger. 'You don't want to believe everything sexy young girls tell you, Ade. The trouble with you is you're too' – she had to search for the word in her limited vocabulary – '*naïve*.'

He tensed. 'So it was deliberate?'

She did not reply. He squinted through half-closed eyes and saw the smirking expression on her face. Just a tart, that was all she was. She was fumbling with his zip. 'Ade . . . couldn't we play a little game, just for fun?'

'What sort of game?' He was suspicious.

'Well, let's pretend we're courtin' again. You and me, out for a Sunday spin and we've stopped 'ere, miles from anywhere. I'm desperate for it and so are you. But I'm safe, just 'ad me monthly, and I want you to do it without usin' anything. Get it?'

'What about *him*?' A nod towards the cot by the van.

'Oh, we 'aven't 'ad 'im. Yet!' She gave a peal of laughter. 'I'm workin' on it!' She had his zip down and was delving inside the open vent. 'Come on, Ade, there's nobody about.'

Damn it, he was letting her undress him. She had confessed to her despicable ruse and now he was going to fall for it again. But he was fully erect, at his weakest. 'We don't want another baby,' he protested feebly, watching her pull her blouse off and begin unfastening her skirt. Her bra was cast to one side, and she was naked. He groaned silently. She had some sort of hold over him, like a spell. It was her body, he could not resist it. 'Hey, we can't afford another!'

'I'm safe, really I am!' She grinned and winked.

A shadow flitted across them and he looked up. A bird. He recognized it as a buzzard, a large hawk. Stately, so wild and free, gliding on those huge ragged wings, flying low. He had never seen one so close before. It passed on out of his range of vision. He envied it its freedom.

Liza was on top of him. She was breathing heavily, her small body shuddering with anticipation even before she guided him into her. Moaning aloud, she was starting to gyrate her shapely hips, head back, eyes closed. He heard that buzzard calling, mewing loudly. It was probably perched somewhere nearby watching them.

There was no way Adrian could stop himself; he felt his orgasm starting and Liza was pressing hard down on him, smirking. *I'm safe, really I am. And you'd believe anything a sexy young girl told you, Ade.*

It was as though his whole body was exploding, convulsing beneath her as she held him down with her slight frame, going with him, one way then the other, sinking down on to him, clawing him with her long fingernails, gasping aloud, shuddering . . . laughing, as if to say, You've done it again, Ade. You've hit the jackpot, like you did before!

Angry with himself as well as her, he wanted to punch her sly face now that the passion was gone from him. *And that was when they heard Sam start to scream.*

They jerked up, still joined, and stared back towards the van. *And there was the buzzard, seemingly the size of a golden eagle, its vicious talons raking the baby, tearing the clothing, ribboning the tender flesh, its wicked curved beak stabbing at the unprotected face.*

Shocked, not even screaming yet, they were robbed

of all movement, just watching in terror, unable to believe what they saw. The baby clothes and cot sheets were spotted crimson. The grotesque winged predator had stripped its victim and was gorging itself on human infant flesh, digging deep, pulling at the tender meat, stringing it into its mouth. An eye was gone, and there was a ragged wound the length of the cheek, and now it was gouging the throat. The baby's yells were growing weaker, becoming a chilling gurgle.

Liza screamed now. She pulled herself free of Adrian, fell, picked herself up, then ran blindly. The buzzard saw her but made no move to flee, just watched her approach with an evil glittering eye. There was not a flicker of fear, just a cold arrogance. Adrian stood dumfounded, a terrified spectator, and saw Liza reach to snatch her child away. *And fell back screaming as those sharp claws tore a strip the length of her arm. The buzzard stabbed deeply at the baby's throat, tore another morsel of meat and swallowed it.*

'Ade, *do* something!'

He found he could move and staggered forward, looking for a weapon; a stick, anything. But there was nothing in sight, and that hooded head was bent over the child again. *You wanted it stillborn, didn't you?* Oh, God Above, he had to save Sam. Please don't kill my baby, he pleaded silently.

Adrian struck at the bird, a sweeping blow that hit it and knocked it sideways in the small transportable cot. It hissed, turned, and as he struck again, it fastened on to his hand with its talons, got a hold on a living perch, and fluttered at his face. Adrian struck blindly at the bird with his other arm, but that beak was too fast for him and bit a finger with the force of a pair of strong garden secateurs. Somehow it had lodged on his bare chest and secured a hold in his flesh. Face to face, he saw those awful malevolent eyes only inches from his own, and then his vision exploded into crimson blindness.

He could not see, heard himself screaming, then felt his attacker flap free; a gigantic wing caught him and sent him reeling; stumbling, falling headlong. Lying on the soft grass, clutching at his bloody sightless eyes, he yelled that he didn't want to be blind. Somewhere, Liza was still screaming. Fuck her, it was all her fault.

Liza had Sam in her arms and cradled his feebly moving bleeding form to her bosom as she fled headlong down the road. The buzzard was behind her, swooping in, pecking, then drawing back. It was driving her, herding her, taunting her in a game of hate. It was in no hurry, keeping pace with her, then wheeling in front and sending her back the other way.

Liza screamed for help. Where were all the cars which cluttered up country lanes at weekends, the picnickers; the bird-watchers? *Sam was limp in her grasp. She almost dropped him as she tried to ward off her attacker's aerial onslaught. The buzzard was like a heavy bomber with the speed and versatility of a midget fighter. She was bleeding from a multitude of wounds, naked and helpless. Weakening.*

Finally she fell, sprawled heavily on the loose chippings and lay there with her baby beneath her, sobbing because she had not the strength to scream any longer. She felt the buzzard alight on her back, secure a foothold in her flesh and begin to feed voraciously on her.

7

'I have to go to London. Today.' There was a note of rare apprehension in John Broughton's voice, like an embarrassed teenager announcing to his parents for the first time that he was going out on a date. Glancing away from his wife's questioning stare, he fidgeted. 'But I should be back first thing tomorrow morning.'

Pamela sighed. 'Do you *have* to go, John?'

'I'm afraid so. Why don't you come along for the trip?' It was a sop, softening the blow, but at the same time he was hoping that she wouldn't accept his invitation. Simply because having Pamela along was an added complication. His time-table went to hell; any arrangements she made would surely clash with his own, they always did.

'Why do you have to go, John?'

'Vogt, the German sporting agent, is in London. We put a lot of business each other's way, I find my clients wild-boar shooting through his agency and he puts all his rich pheasant shooters on to me. He would take it as an insult if I didn't dine with him tonight. But, as I said, you're welcome to join us.'

'How utterly boring.' She drained her coffee cup and pushed it away. 'An evening where the conversation is dominated by the killing of wild animals. No, thank you, all the same.'

'Please yourself, then,' he said abruptly, relieved that she wasn't coming with him but trying not to show it.

'I just wish we had servants living in.' There was a hint of fear in her voice. She hesitated, on the verge of telling him what had happened that night; then changed her mind. It was a long time ago even though sometimes it seemed like yesterday. And everybody knew that the animals were acting strangely.

'It would be nice.' No, it wouldn't because all your privacy would be gone, the house wouldn't be your own. Servants arriving at 7.30 a.m. and departing at 6 p.m. was quite enough for anybody, but Pamela wouldn't see it that way. 'In rural areas it's difficult to get anybody to live in. The days of being in service are long gone.'

'You could advertize.' She was being insistent now.

'I doubt if we'd have much success. Anyway, the staff are adequate.'

'You've got your full-time gamekeeper and that's all you're worried about!' She stood up. 'All right, please yourself, John. See you tomorrow morning.'

She brushed past him, stalked up the stairs. It would be the first time she had been left on her own overnight since . . . *no, don't think about it*. She half-wondered if he had a mistress, some floosie down in London. No, he didn't go often enough and, anyway, workaholics didn't have time for fancy women. Not that she really cared because if he wanted to leave her it would cost him. Plenty. Sometime later she heard the Subaru drive away. She found herself listening, breathing a sigh of relief as she picked up the sound of the vacuum somewhere downstairs. Mrs Bridges, the daily cleaning lady, was still here; she wasn't alone. Yet.

It had been one trauma after another, which was why she resisted the temptation to go for a walk in the warm sunshine. The lad who helped out with the gamekeeping – the hospital said he would be all right now, but anybody was lucky to survive that number of bee-stings. They'd thought he might lose his eyesight but it was returning. However logical one tried to be, there was no getting away from the fact that the creatures of the wild were hellbent on attacking humans; creatures that were normally shy of people had taken on a new boldness, a viciousness. She crossed to the window and closed it. There was a bee on the outside buzzing against the glass. She wasn't chancing its finding a way in. Which was why she was going to stay indoors all day. Boring but safe. She would catch up on a few phone calls, idle chatter which would run up the bill. Blow the bill, she had to talk to somebody.

Pamela realized that she had been dozing in the chair after Mrs Bridges brought her lunch up. The tray and empty plate were gone, so the housekeeper must have crept in and removed it without waking her. She would probably gossip in the village about how the idle rich slept away their days, Pamela thought, but she had been tired, very tired. Now she felt refreshed; which meant that she would not sleep tonight. God, what time was it? Strewth, after seven! Again she found herself listening but there was no sound except the ticking of the grandfather clock down in the hallway. She felt a surge of loneliness, abandonment. Early evening, nearly three hours until darkness fell. And that was when her terror would begin, real or in her imagination.

She should have gone to London with John. Not to that boring dinner – there were dozens of friends she could have visited, or she could even have stayed in the flat. Why the hell hadn't she? Tiredness probably, and the journey was a lot of trouble. Now she was regretting it.

She switched on the television. A soap. She flicked on to another channel. A documentary. About animals. Ugh! Two more choices. She settled for a film but wasn't following it, she had come in in the middle. But it was company, folks talking, moving about. Perhaps she would put the video on all night. At least then she could listen to human voices. Because there was no way she was going to be able to sleep.

Darkness took its time, following a seemingly never-ending summer dusk. Outside blackbirds and thrushes were singing, but when she listened carefully to them there was something not quite *normal* about their eventide shrilling. *Shrilling*, that summed it up, a sort of harshness that bordered on a scream – a hate-filled shriek. *We know you're on your own tonight!* Damn it, her nerves were starting to play up already. She turned up the volume of the television and made sure all the curtains were closed. Had Mrs Bridges locked the doors after her? Surely she had, knowing her mistress was all alone in the house. But it wasn't the housekeeper's job to lock up; as far as Pamela knew, the servant hadn't been instructed to do so. And you didn't start battening down for the night at six, or whenever you left. Not normally. Hell, she would have to go and check.

She switched on the lights as she went, flooding the hallway and then running down the stairs. The front door wasn't locked. Neither was the side door. Nor the back one. Turning keys, shooting bolts home, she ran from room to room. She thought as she ran back upstairs that she had left the kitchen light on. It could bloody well stop on until morning then.

There, that was it, everywhere barred and bolted. Hard luck, you bastards, you're stopping outside tonight. *Unless, of course, they were already inside!*

Fear balling her stomach, she glanced round the bedroom. There was a bluebottle buzzing round the lightshade – there always was, wherever you were in summer. She could either spray some fly-killer and breathe in the pungent fumes half the night or else embark upon a frustrating chase with a rolled-up newspaper. She wasn't going to do either. She would take a bath, a long, leisurely one.

Pamela felt safer in the bathroom. She checked the bolt a second time to make sure it was firmly in place before she turned on the taps, opened a sachet of herbal bathfoam and dropped the contents into the water, watching it become a green foam. Only then did she slip out of her housecoat. Yes, this was the safest place in the house, nowhere for anything to hide; no way anything could get at her, and the window was opaque glass so that those beastly moths tapping on the pane could not see in, not even through a gap in the curtains. She would order a roller blind for this window, much more fashionable.

She stretched out in the warm frothy water, relaxed for possibly the first time since John had announced that he was going away, in a world of her own. She would stop here for an hour, maybe two. Perhaps all night. If she kept topping up with warm water there was no reason why she shouldn't. It was more comfortable than the bed. And so much safer.

Accidentally she touched her body beneath the water and thrilled to the sensation. Her fingertips moved again, rubbed sensuously, and she moaned softly. It was a long time since she had done anything like this. An awful long time since she had enjoyed any sexual pleasure at all. Because John was too busy, too tired when he came to bed. Or she was. A ready-made excuse that had become permanent. But she wasn't thinking of her husband right now; he was so boring. In her mind she saw a handsome olive-skinned man with wavy dark hair, heard his voice whisper in her ear. Persuasive, seductive. She groaned again and closed her eyes so that she might see him better. The memory was more vivid now; two years ago but it might only have been last night. Or tonight. A nobody from a working-class background, and his rep's job depended upon commission, which was probably why he had learned to be persuasive, to talk people into doing things against their better judgement. Women mostly. Like herself.

John had been abroad on a business trip; she had slummed it and gone back with Roland to his flat, a crummy one-bedroomed apartment in Camden Town. God, it was so erotic there, far more than ever it could have been in her own Mayfair suite. Sleazy screwing; she had begged him to leave the light on so that she could see her surroundings. And Roland. Whatever his pedigree, he knew what a woman liked most. Clutching at him because she was starting to orgasm and she might take off, spinning crazily, she cried her delight aloud. She was still holding on to the bed as he came away from her . . . holding on to the side of the bath as the ornate ceiling became distorted, shimmering through the steam. *And that was when she saw the spider.*

It was a big one. Huge. It perched effortlessly above the light fitting, upside down on the ceiling, and moved a leg just to let her know it was alive. But it was the eyes that frightened her most. That and the fact that it was watching her. There was no doubt about that.

Twin pinpoints shone greenly, reflecting the herbal tint of the bathwater. Staring unblinking, its gaze focused on her. She tensed, pressing herself against the side of the bath, and heard the water slop over the sides. She had never seen a spider's eyes before, never realized that they had eyes, although logically they had to or else they would not have been able to see. Or a spider's face, either, with screwed up little features that looked like a shirt button with cracks all over it. But those orbs dominated, bored right into her, hating her, mocking her for what she had just done. Civilized and yet you can't do without *that*! It seemed to be laughing in its own revolting insect way, sensing her fear of a creature thousands of times smaller than herself. It moved and for a moment it was lost from her view behind the lightshade. Then she saw it again, suspended on a thread which it might have made long ago in readiness for this moment, lowering itself down two or three inches. It stopped, hanging there. *I'm coming down but there's no hurry. Just lie where you are and I'll land right on you. Crawl all over you.*

No! She sat up, slipped and slid, sending another frothy wave over the side. She had a sudden fear that she might not be able to get out of the bath, like one of those awful nightmares where, try as you would, you never got anywhere. The spider dropped another inch and swung like a pendulum, still watching her.

Those moths were hammering crazily against the outside of the window, pinging incessantly in their frenzy. There was a dull thump as something heavier struck the glass, then fluttered. She knew what it was and almost screamed. A bat! But it couldn't get in, could it?

They were going crazy out there, like a living hailstorm pattering on the window. Desperate to get to her. Like the spider.

It dropped down another couple of inches.

Pamela made it out of the bath and slid over the side, thighs wide and upended for a second before she landed on the bathmat. Those twin orbs glowed with lust. It saw and understood. *I'm going to crawl there as well.* Oh, God!

She snatched up a towel and wrapped it round herself, inhibited and terrified. An insect voyeur! She would kill it. How? She searched wildly for a weapon with her eyes: sponge, soap, a loofa. Nothing solid. It gyrated, then came down still further. It was within reach now but she wasn't going to touch it. Ugh!

Outside the assault on the toughened glass (she prayed that it was toughened) had reached an intensity beyond belief. An army of winged creatures battered themselves insanely against it, and there was the deeper thud of the bat; there might even have been two of them. Or three. Bloodsuckers waiting to join the spider. A cacophony of tiny squeakings joined the background of buzzing. Mosquitoes; they sucked blood, too. She was on the verge of panic.

She dropped the towel and slid into her housecoat. I've got to get out, back to the bedroom, she thought. But they'll only follow me; the spider will scuttle across the landing, squeeze under the door. The bats and moths will flit across to another window. Light attracts them. But I'm not sitting in the dark, not with *that*.

That loathsome spider was alighting on the taps, squatting there. She turned, snatched at the bolt, pulled the door open and slammed it after her, rolling a mat up against it. But it didn't fit snugly enough, it might not even hinder her pursuer. She fled for the bedroom.

The bats beat her to it. They were flapping at the window even as she entered, those shrill squeaks much louder now. The glass was buffeted, it might crack at any second. Shatter and . . .

The curtains wafted where some summer breeze infiltrated, opening up a gap of an inch or so, like the finale of a play where the audience were afforded one last glimpse of the cast. This time Pamela screamed as she saw the repulsive tiny faces pressed up against the glass, almost human in their expressions, sheer malevolence as pairs of tiny eyes burned their hate at her. *We'll get you, make no mistake about that. Time is on our side. Before daylight the glass will break and . . .*

She made up her mind then that she was going to leave the house. The curtain fell back into place. Thankfully she could only hear them now. With trembling hands she pulled on a pair of Levis and a checked shirt, and had difficulty in lacing up her pumps. Glancing towards the door all the time, she was expecting at any second to see that revolting squat shape come squeezing under the gap beneath it, eyes fixed on her. *We know what you did in the bath. You're no better than us. An animal.*

She paused. The Justy was out there, backed up to the front door. Unlocked. She had the ignition keys in her hand. Shaking, she wondered if there was an alternative. There wasn't. She had to run a gauntlet of maybe ten yards. *They* would know, of course. Even now they might be massing in ambush outside the door, waiting for her to emerge, a cloud of fluttering, swooping, biting creatures after her blood. But if she stayed here they would get to her before daylight, so she had to make a run for it.

Creeping to the head of the stairs, she glanced back at the bathroom door but there was still no sign of the spider. If John had been here he would have killed it as mercilessly as he slew pheasant on shoot days. It wouldn't have stood a chance. But he wasn't here and . . . *she saw it coming, crawling up over the rolled-up doormat, oozing its rubbery body back into shape and seeing her.* That was when she ran, full flight across the hallway.

There was not a sound to be heard at the door, not

so much as the droning of a nightmoth. And the silence was a thousand times more chilling.

She pulled open the door and saw the Justy glinting there in the porch light, waiting for her. She ran, leaving the front door swinging behind her, not caring if these creatures of the night infiltrated the big house, because she wasn't coming back.

She made it to the car, dragged the door wide, threw herself into the driver's seat and slammed it behind her. Seconds later they hit the windows and pattered on the shiny metalwork, seething their buzzing and squeaking, angry because she had beaten them to it with seconds to spare. A mass of revolting tiny bodies clustered on the windscreen; she started the wipers and cut a swathe through them. They flew off, came back, and were swept away again.

Thank God, the engine fired first time. She switched on the headlights, and the full beam showed a cloud of flying insects homing in on the car; the bats were jinking and weaving, dive-bombing.

Only now did she give a thought to her destination. Where, for Christ's sake, in this rural area where the inhabitants went to bed at dark? And where she knew virtually nobody. Except the gamekeeper and his wife, the Shanks. There was nowhere else, and they would understand.

Even as she let in the clutch insects of innumerable species were covering the windscreen, obscuring her vision, in a concerted effort to prevent her escape. The wipers struggled to move them, the screen-washer attempting to clear the squashed corpses, but the glass was still blood-streaked as the car pulled away. Peering through the mulch, the swarming bodies, she drove slowly so that she could see the track. Stones were thrown up and banged on the underside of the vehicle. She switched on the radio, turning it up to full volume in an attempt to shut out the drone of those awful predators.

A mile, probably less, to the Shanks' cottage. She wondered if she would make it before her attackers clogged the engine and brought the car to a halt. And if that happened it was only a matter of time before they found a way inside. She felt herself starting to panic but fought it off with a determined effort. And all the time her visibility was being reduced until she could see barely more than ten yards ahead.

8

John Broughton experienced an immense relief at being away from the Corby estate. He also felt a nagging guilt at having left Pamela behind; strange things were happening, there was no getting away from that. But his wife would be all right if she stayed indoors, as she undoubtedly would. Damn it, they weren't going to let the bloody animals take over. No, there had to be a logical explanation, an aftermath of Chernobyl or something like that. But it wasn't happening anywhere else in the area; just Corby. Which sent a little shiver up his spine. When he returned he would check with the tenant farmers, ascertain what chemicals they were spraying on their crops. Not that he was going to advocate a return to organic growing or anything as obsessional as that. In the meantime he had some important business to transact. The sporting potential of his new lands had to be exploited to the full. And if the wildlife continued to be a threat then the lot would be exterminated and he would start from scratch. One way or another the problem would be overcome.

Erich Vogt was blond-haired and slightly overweight, and bore the hallmark of a man who enjoyed the good things in life. At forty-two he was reputedly one of the best shots in West Germany, both at pheasant drives with his sixteen-bore and at wild boar with a 9 mm rifle. Confident, abrasive by nature, he needed careful handling. Offend him and he would call a deal off whether it was to his advantage or not. One had to be diplomatic but not humble, because the sporting agent despised weakness.

'And how are your pheasants doing, Mr Broughton?' The question was far from casual. His clients expected the best, the highest birds, and he would not tolerate complaints of badly shown game.

'Fine.' Broughton sipped his cognac and dropped his gaze. Too bloody good, he thought they'd claw you to death if they got the chance. 'I am confident of providing some of the best sport in England this next season.'

'Good, good.' Fleshy hands were rubbed together. 'But I know that I can rely upon you where shooting is concerned. My clients have been very satisfied in the past. But it is not about shooting which I wish to talk to you tonight.'

'Oh?' With a sense of apprehension, Broughton took another sip of brandy.

'I want to know if you can provide some of my most exclusive customers with fishing. Trout, of course. I understand that you also have fishing on the Corby estate.'

'That's right, a good mile of trout river. Both banks.'

'And the sporting potential?'

'It promises well although we have been busy concentrating on the pheasants up until now. But I shall certainly be stocking the river. There are some nice trout in it, anyway. I think that next season should be good.'

'Then we can do business.' The German's eyes narrowed. 'Tell me, Mr Broughton, we have read some strange things about Corby in our own newspapers.'

'Oh!' John thought the caviare was starting to curdle in his stomach. 'You mean about animals acting strangely? Well, the press always exaggerate, don't they? A woman was bitten by an adder, our part-time keeper was attacked by wild bees. Yes, I agree it was unfortunate, bad publicity, but everything is under control.'

God I hope so. He wondered what Pamela was doing right now. Probably locked in the bedroom watching television.

'Yes, bad publicity.' Vogt's expression was stoic. 'But it is also bad for business. My clients are wealthy, they can shoot or fish where they please. One whisper that something is amiss, that there is danger, and they will go elsewhere. You understand me, don't you?'

'Yes.' There was a hint of a tremor in John's voice. 'But I can't help it if the papers blow up some trivial happening, can I?'

'You must take steps to see that there are no adverse trivial happenings.' It was a direct order. 'I have my reputation to consider too, Mr Broughton. Not only this season's shooting but the fishing to follow is at stake. I am sure you will see that all is well. Now, I would like to send one of my field managers to take a look at your river and weigh up the possibilities. The earlier the better. Shall we say Monday week?'

'Yes, that will be fine.' Broughton's reply was instantaneous. Where Vogt was concerned, he who hesitated was definitely lost. 'I'll fix it up as soon as I get back home.'

'I knew I could rely on you.' The German laughed throatily, humourlessly, and signalled to the wine waiter to bring more brandies. Vintage ones at thirty pounds a glass; extravagance was incidental where deals of this calibre were concerned.

The wipers were managing to keep a small triangular section of the windscreen relatively clear of the swarming nocturnal insects. It was smeared with blood and squashed corpses but at least Pamela Broughton had a restricted field of vision, enough to keep her on the rough track. The headlights were dim, full beam little more powerful than the sidelights as tiny fluttering bodies adhered to the glass, three deep sometimes. Those dislodged by the airstream of the moving Justy were instantly replaced.

The engine missed, then picked up. She caught her breath, aware that she was sweating heavily. *God, suppose I break down! Don't think about it, just keep going.*

The screenwash bottle was empty; the wiper blades were squeaking as they forced their way round the rapidly diminishing arc with no lubrication apart from the blood of the moths which they trapped, creating a build-up like they did in driving snow. But there was no way she was going to pull up and get out to clear the wedge of tiny bodies. Surely she could not be all that far from the Shanks' cottage now?

There was a thud as a bat hurled itself at the glass screen, the impact cushioned by the milling insects. It dropped on to the bonnet and fluttered on its back. That's done for you, you little bugger, she thought. No, the bat rolled over, perched there, flew off into the darkness. It would be back shortly; if not this one then another.

There was something crawling on her face. She slapped at it and felt a tiny body crunch. It was stuck to her fingers but she managed to flick it away. She was afraid now because that insect, whatever it was, had found a way inside the car. There might be others waiting to settle on her, to bite her. She tried to listen for them but it was impossible to hear anything above the drone of those outside and the noise of the engine, which stuttered again, then jerked. She dared not think how many living bodies were clustered beneath the bonnet.

Suddenly she was braking. There was an animal standing in the track; at first, through the streaked windscreen, she thought it was a cow. No, it wasn't the right shape, too lean and the horns were different, like tree branches. A deer, a stag! She blasted the horn; it sounded muffled, more like a squeak. And the stag did not move, just stood there facing her.

'Get out of the way or I'll run you down!' she shouted, but heard her whispered voice in the enclosed space. Down to five m.p.h. Then at a standstill. The engine ticked over erratically, threatening to die.

The animal turned and faced the car, head lowered. It eyes glinted in the wan glow of the headlights and there was no mistaking its fury. Pamela recoiled, pressing herself back in her seat. Oh, my God, she thought, it's going to *charge*! There was a sudden eerie silence. *The insects swarming over the vehicle were no longer buzzing and droning. It was as though they had forced the Justy to a halt, brought her here at the mercy of this beast of the forest.*

She wondered if the car would stand the impact. The stag looked huge. There were a couple of signs on the main road warning motorists to beware of deer. Surely it wouldn't be strong enough to wreck a vehicle, just do some damage perhaps. Something was crawling on her chin. She swatted it and felt a sticky morass adhering to her palm. Merciful heaven, those dreadful flying things *were* finding a means of entrance. She reached across and slammed the fresh air vent shut just to be on the safe side.

The engine stuttered again. And died.

An impact shook the car, causing things to spill out of the open glove box. Something was rolling and clinking on the floor. Glass shattered – one of the headlights. Now her visibility was even less. The wipers struggled to keep the only means of vision clear, screeching their dried-up progress. I don't want to see, she thought.

Trying not to panic, she turned the ignition key and pumped the accelerator pedal . . . a whine that died away. She tried it again. This time it fired reluctantly and she revved, getting it going again, with a sudden burst of power as if an obstruction had cleared.

The stag was backing off, lowering its antlers again. It saw a rival at the rutting stand and was maddened by its presence, a robot foe which had to be vanquished. The beast charged and Pamela braced herself for the impact.

Much harder this time. The car was pushed back a foot or so and there was a grinding of metal. The creature was caught up somewhere; probably its antlers were wedged in the radiator grill. It was twisting, ripping, pushing and pulling. Miraculously the engine was still running. Pamela revved again, her own roar of protest drowning that of her attacker. A snapping sound, and the stag fell back, momentarily lost its footing and rolled in the track, throwing up a cloud of dust as if to screen its ignominious fall.

The Justy shot forward; she had not meant to drive at the creature but her left foot slipped off the clutch, propelling the car rather than stalling it. There was a sickening thump. The beast reared, screamed in pain and leaped to one side. Driving blindly for a few seconds, she caught the stag again as she passed it, hearing it shriek its agony and fury a second time. The wiper picked up speed and she could see again. No way was she going to stop now, not until she reached the gamekeeper's cottage.

Now there was a concerted attack by her winged pursuers. She sensed their outrage at her defiance as missiles splatted against the side windows when her sudden burst of speed took her through them. Bumping over potholes, dimly she recognized the place where Peach had died, where . . . oh, no! *There was a badger scuttling in front of her, a grey and black striped head turned in her direction. Perhaps the very one that had mauled her poodle to death*!

Stopping, dazzled by the restricted beam of the single headlamp, it crouched in her path. Instinctively her foot went to the brake pedal but she snatched it away. She could have swerved, gone on to the edge of the grassy field and back again; a swift detour that might have avoided a collision. But suddenly her own fury was aroused, her hate for an animal that had killed needlessly, against its very nature. For a brief second she saw Peach again, the mangled, pathetic body. Oh, Christ, she owed him this!

Instead of braking or swerving, she slammed her foot hard down on the throttle pedal. She felt the Justy respond and hurtle forward. The badger made no move to leap for the safety of the verge. And then it was lost to view. She felt a wheel bump, and the car slewed on the dry, dusty surface. It stalled, stopped, the badger wedged underneath it. Again the engine fired and she crashed the gears into reverse, backing, jerking free of the corpse that had jammed its progress. *Oh, no, the badger wasn't dead*!

Somehow it hauled itself back on to its feet, blood pouring from a wide gash in its hairy side. Half of its face seemed to have gone, leaving just a mulch out of which a single eye glared balefully. It was staggering, trying to escape, then it flopped down again. You bastard, she thought. That was what happened to Peach. Now you know what it feels like!

She gunned the engine and drove hard at the wounded creature, guiding the nearside wheels so that they went directly over her victim. Not euthanasia – vengeance! One prolonged scream that was almost human embodied the ultimate in pain and suffering; a soft squelch. The bile came up and burned her throat as she envisaged the gashed side crumpling, the abdomen ballooning and shooting out a morass of bloody entrails. She retched, then laughed aloud hysterically. *I got you. I bloody well got you! And that was for Peach*!

The bats were back again, three of them dive-bombing the windscreen with a renewed obsession, bouncing off the toughened glass, oblivious to injury, one with a broken wing hanging on to the smooth glass and seeping blood, which the wiper spread in a crimson arced swathe. Now two, that damaged one finally losing its grip and disappearing. Pamela laughed and the sound frightened her. *But I'm leaving a trail of dead and dying in my wake!*

With relief she saw the cottage amidst the tall pines fifty yards away. She had made it! The covering of insects on windscreen and windows had thinned, as if even they had realized the hopelessness of their cause. The gate was open. She peered in an attempt to see the parked Land Rover but it was nowhere in sight. Possibly it was at the rear of the building. She slowed to a halt but kept the engine running, her unease mounting as she saw that all the windows were in darkness. A feeling of loneliness, abandonment, came over her. If the Shanks were not at home then she was trapped in the furthermost part of the Corby estate; the main road lay in the opposite direction and she would have to drive back through all . . . *that* again. And at that moment the Justy's engine petered out. She made no attempt to restart it because she knew that this time it was gone for good. Dead.

She sat there in the dim glow of the facia lights. The remaining headlight was beginning to fade. Eventually there would be just pitch blackness and outside . . . Don't be bloody stupid, she told herself, Jill and the children are probably in bed and Gordon is out on patrol somewhere. Jill had told her how he regularly spent the night hours patrolling the estate, guarding his pheasants. He might be back shortly.

Pamela pressed the horn. There was a barely audible response. She sighed. It was probably jammed full of dead and dying moths. There was no point in getting out, she would be at the mercy of the creatures of darkness. She'd just sit here and wait for the gamekeeper to return, or for daylight, whichever came first. She looked at the clock on the dashboard and groaned her despair aloud. 2.15 a.m. She didn't know what time it got light, she had not seen a dawn for years, had had no wish to until now. And then she heard the soft tapping of the insects on the glass again. They had not given up after all.

She thought about shouting, but in order to attract the sleeping occupants' attention she would need to wind a window down. She shuddered and gave up the idea. But there was nobody in the cottage. She knew that, sensed the emptiness.

Slowly her anger began to manifest itself. Why the hell wasn't the gamekeeper here? It was his job to be around the place. A full-time servant, he had no business going off somewhere when he was needed. He had taken advantage of John's absence, the old adage that when the cat was away.... *Something was moving out there, rubbing itself against the side of the car. Oh, no, I can't stand any more!*

She felt its progress, whatever it was, a hairy thing that scraped its way along the sill from the rear past the driver's door. So *close*. It was breathing heavily, a kind of snorting; stopping, then moving on again. Now it was at the front, up against the damaged bumper, using it like a kind of scratching post, grunting. A pig, maybe. Did the Shanks keep pigs? She didn't know, didn't care, because every animal was an enemy now.

Then she caught a glimpse of the creature as it moved a yard or so away from the car and she shrieked her terror aloud. *No, it could not be, it was impossible, against all the laws of Nature! The animal had dragged itself clear of the vehicle as if deliberately revealing its presence, its identity, to her. A squat form, its coarse hair matted with blood, barely recognizable except for that yawning gash in its side, its guts spilling out of it like a nest of crimson vipers, and a single malevolent eye blazing its hate for mankind in the pulped head. The badger, the one which Pamela Broughton had run down in revenge for the killing of her poodle, had no right to be alive*

She jerked her head away, fought against being forced to look upon that hideous thing. It was grunting again. The chilling liquid noises sounded as if it was gurgling its last. But it was dead back there, half a mile down the road, there was no way it could possibly have survived!

She sank down on the seat, covered her eyes and trembled because the bats were knocking on the windows again. *We'll get you in the end, you can't hide in there forever. You'll have to come out or die because nobody's going to come to your rescue.*

They will. The gamekeeper will be back soon, she thought.

No, he won't. He's gone. For good.

Crying softly, she was in despair now. If the badger had returned from the dead then surely that stag would come back too and buffet the car in an unrelenting anger from beyond the grave. Cringing, she braced herself for the inevitable charge, for those wicked antlers which would twist the bodywork open like an avenging crowbar.

The insects were noisier than ever now, their steady drone rising in a macabre crescendo, their hum vibrating the metalwork of the Justy. Gathering for the final onslaught, they would break through by sheer weight of numbers like a cloud of hungry locusts that nothing could withstand. Hands clasped to her ears, she was trying to shut everything out. *Just let me die and get it over with*!

Something banged on the door. Pamela jumped, then dragged herself across on to the passenger seat, as far away as the cramped space of the small car would allow. It was the stag. She had been anticipating its return, and now it was here. Injured like the badger, a dying beast of vengeance, it was preparing to charge. The animal battering ram, oblivious to pain, was gouging and tearing at the buckled metal until it reached her. Then it would impale her on its wicked horns, dragging her, goring her, holding the remains of her bloody body aloft, the death prize for all the maddened creatures of this accursed place to view with pride and hatred. The first death; but there would be many more.

The doorhandle was being tried, rattled. No, I don't believe it! A light dazzled her even though her eyes were firmly closed. There was a knocking on the window; it was going to smash the glass with its antlers! It would succeed where the bats and insects had failed.

Pamela screamed and buried her face in the upholstery. *I'm not going to look, I don't want to see*!

'*Open up*!' A voice, words, impinged on her bemused brain. Crazy. Even crazier than creatures that died and lived again, she thought, trying to shut the voice out. It spoke again. 'Hey, open the door.'

With slow realization came an hysterical giggling. Recognizing the features of the young gamekeeper in the glare of the torchlight, she fumbled with the doorlock and eventually released it. Allowing herself to be helped out, she tried to warn him of the creatures that lurked in ambush in the surrounding darkness. More voices – tired children, and one that she recognized as belonging to Jill Shank.

Finally the relief was too much for Pamela Broughton and she fainted.

9

Gordon Shank had a worried expression on his face for a number of reasons. First, the boss was back and the pressure was on now. It was the old story of passing the buck and the keeper ended up with it. Gordon had taken Pamela back to the big house, and it was almost as if John Broughton was blaming him for what had happened.

'Jesus, not *again*!' Broughton stood there, hands on hips, his anger visibly building up inside him. 'Badgers, foxes, snakes, stags, bees, what else? I think we'll have to do some culling. Fast!'

'Deer are out of season,' Gordon replied, then wished that he had not spoken.

'I don't give a shit whether they're in or out of season. Shoot every one you can find. Badgers too. What became of the injured ones that made such a mess of the Justy?'

'Nowhere to be found.'

'They have to be. Get your dogs on their scent.'

'I already have. There was some blood and hairs, spoor leading away from the spot where Pamela hit them. Then nothing. Just like their animal friends have hid 'em, buried 'em or something.'

'That's bloody ridiculous!' Broughton snapped. 'They can't have got far. Still, those particular ones are probably dead by now. It's the live ones we have to worry about. Better get plenty of snares out, catch up the badgers, too.'

'I can't do that. I daren't, they're protected. You can go to jail for persecuting badgers. You know that as well as I do. And the law doesn't even have to prove it now under the Wildlife and Countryside Act. Suspicion is enough, you're guilty till you're proved innocent, contrary to every other aspect of British law. It's more than my job's worth. I'd never get another. Be reasonable.'

'Then *I'll* kill the bastards personally!' John glanced at the damaged car, which had been towed back up to the house, then raised his eyes to the bedroom window. Pamela was in bed, sleeping off her trauma. In all probability she would insist on going back to live in Mayfair. And all because of a few bloody animals. They were bad for business, too. Which reminded him of his meeting with Vogt.

'By the way, I've got a job for you on Monday week, Gordon. Vogt is sending one of his field managers over here. Yes, I know he'll be a bloody nuisance when we're not only busy but we've got all kinds of problems. But there's nothing I can do about it and if I put him off the Germans will get suspicious. He wants to check the river over with a view to sending fishermen over here next season. What are the trout like?'

'To tell you the truth I haven't been near the river for a fortnight. Damn it, we've got pheasants near to release that are giving us all kinds of headaches. I haven't even given the river a thought.'

'Then you'd better get down there and take a look. And don't tell me the damned fish are out to get us, too!' It was meant to be a joke but suddenly it wasn't very funny. If the animals on the Corby estate were after human blood, then why should the fish act any differently, John thought. But, he consoled himself, at least the fish couldn't leave the water.

'I'll find an hour to have a look.' The gamekeeper turned towards his Land Rover. 'Okay, we'll increase the fox wires, but it won't be easy finding the time to check them twice daily. Since young Simpson got attacked by the bees I've had it all to do single-handed.'

'What about your boy, isn't he helping you weekends and evenings?'

Gordon hesitated. It wasn't fair to rope Gary in even if the lad was enthusiastic about helping. Slave labour; and Jill didn't like their son going off on his own these days. 'Jill isn't keen.' He had learned to pass the buck like everybody else. 'Not after . . . all that's happened.'

'I'll pay him, how's that?'

'I'll put it to Jill.'

'If he carries his gun he'll be all right.'

They regarded each other steadily, both of them recalling how the pheasant poults had mobbed the boy in the release pen. But he hadn't had his gun handy; a shot had soon sent them packing. Gordon nearly reminded his employer that Gary wasn't legally old enough to carry a gun without supervision. He thought better of it; they weren't playing the game by the book any longer. 'All right, I'll see what I can do.'

Which meant that Gary was the new part-time keeper. There was no way they would be able to stop the boy, short of locking him in his bedroom. All the same, it was worrying.

Jill Shank hated weekends more than ever now. Previously their son had helped Gordon, but it had been a kind of learning job, an apprenticeship that entailed the boy accompanying his father on his rounds. Now it was different. Broughton was paying a wage and Gary was expected to earn it; if Gordon took the lad with him then they were not, in effect, getting through extra work. It needed one to tend the pheasants, the other to concentrate on vermin control.

'Isn't Gary back yet?' Jill was tense as she called through to her husband from the kitchen. Breakfast was almost ready. The keepers had been up since daylight and Gordon was just back from feeding the penned pheasants. Gary had gone up to Spion Kop to look at some fox snares.

'He won't be long,' Gordon called back. 'I heard a shot about twenty minutes ago.'

'Oh, my God!' She took the frying pan off the stove and appeared in the doorway, maternal concern in her expression.

'Don't panic,' Gordon laughed, slipping his jacket off. 'He carries his gun, he's bound to shoot sometimes – that's what it's for. I hope it was a fox in a wire. One less!'

'And I hope so, too.' She went back to the stove, heard footsteps outside on the yard and called, 'Is that you, Gary?' There was no mistaking the tension in her voice.

'Yeah.' His excitement bordered on euphoria. 'Come and see what I've got, Mum.'

'I can't.' She didn't want to see. So long as her son was all right, it didn't matter what he'd shot. She heard Gordon going outside. Men! It made no difference if the breakfast got cold when some gamekeeping topic cropped up. Damn it, Gary didn't have to bring his latest exhibit back here, he could have left it up in the woods like Gordon did. But the boy was proud of himself; it would be unfair to dishearten him.

'It's a big 'un.' Gary stood with one foot on the dead badger, the noose around its neck biting deep into the coarse hair where he had dragged it back across the fields.

'God!' Gordon grimaced. 'I wish you hadn't brought it home, laddie. We'll have to bury it. If anybody sees this . . .'

'Mr Broughton said to kill every badger we can.' There was disappointment on the young features at the anticlimax. 'He told me so himself. An extra fifty pence for every brock dead.'

'It's all right for him to say that,' Gordon groaned, 'but it's us that carries the can if we get caught. All right, we'll bury it after breakfast . . . hey, just a minute!'

The gamekeeper dropped to one knee, turned the badger over and saw the gaping wound in its side, the terrible disfiguration of the long head. Ghastly injuries, but the blood had dried, congealed. 'How long ago did you shoot it, Gary?'

'Quarter of an hour, maybe twenty minutes. Why?'

'These wounds. . . .'

'They were on it when I found it. It was pulling and scratching in the snare. It had scraped out a hole nearly as big as itself and when it heard me coming it was straining to get at me. Looks like it's been hit by a car or something.'

'You can say that again!' The keeper straightened up. Suddenly the morning wasn't warm any more; it was decidedly chilly, goosepimpling his skin. That badger had been run over, all right. In all probability by a Subaru Justy. Pamela's kill. But the animal had survived against all odds, against all the laws of Nature, wounded, maddened, and still lusting to kill until a charge of shot at close range had finally despatched it. 'We'd better go in to breakfast or else your mother will get cross.'

'Can I have a go at the crows on the laid barley?' Gary had finished his bacon and eggs and was already starting on the toast. 'As I came back down from the home covert there were thousands of them. You must've heard 'em, Dad. Mr Yates will be complaining to the boss that we're not protecting his crops if we don't do something about them.'

Gordon smiled. The boy had worked hard on the tedious chores, an hour or two shooting crows would do him good, teach him to handle that gun of his. It was far more skilful than blasting badgers and foxes caught in snares. But he'd tell him grudgingly, make it sound like a treat, otherwise the boy would always want to be off with the gun. 'I don't know. There's an awful lot of feeding round to be done, traps and snares to check.'

'Aw, Dad, I've done the snares. And the traps up in the big wood. There's only the two smaller lots of birds to feed. You've done the big pen yourself.'

The boy was shrewd, getting the hang of their routine far better than John Simpson had ever done. 'All right, just until lunch time, then.'

'Lunch will be early.' Jill spoke quickly, perhaps too quickly. 'I want to go shopping in Stratford this afternoon. Claire needs some new clothes for school.'

'She isn't even up yet.' Gary glanced scornfully in the direction of the stairs.

'Which has nothing whatever to do with going shopping this afternoon!' Cool it, she told herself. You're getting edgy. 'Lunch will be at twelve. Sharp.'

'I could take some sandwiches with me.'

'No you can't!' she snapped. 'I want you back here for midday, or else you don't go in the first place. Got it?'

The boy glanced at his father. Gordon nodded in agreement with Jill. Midday and no later.

'And you can go easy on the cartridges, too. Only shoot at those birds in range. There's some crow decoys in the shed, an owl too. See how you get on with them. Use the call like I've taught you.'

'Thanks, Dad.' Gary got up from the table, eating his last round of toast and marmalade as he went. 'And I'll be back for twelve. I promise.'

It was going to be very hot in an hour or two, Gary decided, as he sweated his way up to the grassy slope which led up to Yates's cornfield. The bag of decoys weighed heavy on his shoulder, the lightweight twenty-bore seemed a couple of pounds heavier than it had been when he had gone the rounds of the fox snares before breakfast. His clothes were clinging clammily to his body; if you were going decoying then you had to wear a camouflage jacket and broad-brimmed hat to match. A mesh face mask, too, to screen the whiteness of your features, which the corvines would spot half a mile away. Warm work on a day like today but he wasn't complaining.

A flock of rooks rose up out of the corn, where they had been feeding on an area laid flat by a heavy thunderstorm a fortnight ago. Cawing their displeasure at this interruption of their breakfast, wheeling, their harsh calling seemed somehow more than just irritation; hatred for the human who clambered over the stile. It was all in the mind, Gary thought. Crows were crows; they made that din wherever you found them, not just on the estate.

The birds flew round, then dispersed. In a couple of minutes there wasn't a single one in sight. They had probably returned to the wood, or perhaps another field; he hoped they would not decide to spend the rest of the day there. No, they'd be back, this was the best patch of barley in the area.

He laid his gun down, walked out some thirty yards to where the corn lay flat on the ground and began placing the lifelike rubber crows the way his father had taught him: beaks to the wind. There was not so much as a breeze today so maybe it didn't matter. Pushing the spring-loaded support pegs into the ground, he noted how the imitation black birds bobbed on the ends. Standing back to survey his handiwork, he thought they looked the real McCoy.

Just the owl now. Another rubber dummy, huge yellow eyes and a hooked beak, it looked . . . evil! But at least an artificial bird couldn't attack you. *Don't be bloody stupid*! He walked back to the hedge, bent over a tall branch and fixed the remaining decoy on it, then let the bough spring back into place. The predator bobbed on the top, a foot or so above the dense foliage, in full view of any passing crow. Crows had an obsession with hawks, an inbuilt hatred so that they massed and mobbed any unfortunate one they came across: owls, sparrowhawks, kestrels, buzzards, it mattered not. Natural foes, it was a kind of bullying, sadistic game, but it never ended in a kill because birds of prey were too fierce for a close encounter.

Gary found himself a place of ambush, a gap in the hedge with enough foliage to break up the outline of his crouched body, and slipped a cartridge into the breach of his shotgun. He was tense with anticipation, fingering the call which hung from a leather thong around his neck. It sounded indistinguishable from the call of living corvines if you blew it right; the sound, combined with the sight of a hated owl, had the birds coming to investigate, for once unwary. If you kept still and shot only at those in range, it was possible to make a killing. *Come on, you buggers, where the hell have you got to?*

He checked his watch. Nine-thirty. Two and a half hours until his mother would be serving up lunch. He had better pack up at a quarter to twelve just to be on the safe side; he had a feeling that this time she had meant what she said.

It was hotter than ever. Nine-fifty and still no sign of a crow. He was tempted to blow his call. No, you only answered when a corvine called. Maybe they had decided to feed somewhere else after all.

A sudden rush of wings, low and close, and he caught a brief glimpse of the bird which had glided silently down the hedgerow, swooped and wheeled, but only called when it veered and was lost to his view. Blast it! The gun was half-raised, then lowered again. Perhaps, he thought, it was a scout sent to check out the owl, and had gone back to report to the others. Gary was eager now, straining his eyes through the mesh of the face mask. Then he heard the crows coming, their harsh, hateful screeching as they singled out their enemy atop the hawthorn hedge.

A dozen of them were wheeling, maybe suspicious or just cautious because owls had sharp talons. Gary put the call to his lips and blew twice. The birds answered in chorus and came straight in.

He fired. Too hasty in his eagerness, he knew he had missed even as he squeezed the trigger. The deafening report silenced the corvines temporarily, making them back-pedal in alarm. Cursing, he ejected the spent shell and pushed another cartridge into the breech. Only then was he aware that something was not quite right and tried to work out what it was.

The startled birds had not fled! They bunched, circled and called raucously, and in the distance he heard an answering clamour. The big flock was on its way in response to a corvine summons for help.

Gary Shank was uneasy. He sweated behind his mask and watched the first lot of crows carefully. They were cunning enough to keep just out of range; they knew but they were not afraid. A kind of reconaissance party, shotgun fodder if necessary, they had been sent to draw the fire of the human who had set up this ambush of death. He remembered those pheasants that day, the way they had gone berserk and attacked him. He licked his dry lips and waited. If he had not had a gun he would have run.

One bird swooped in towards the decoys. Gary fired again, and this time he saw his target fall, gliding towards the ground, one wing folded, the other flapping. A hit but not a kill. The wounded bird crashed on to the corn, then stood up. And watched him, its black eyes brimful of sheer evil, its beak open and cursing him for what he had done. Its incessant, crazed screeching was urging its companions to swarm in for the kill!

A flapping of wings from behind, and a near silent attacker had him ducking and shooting in panic. And missing. A crow chorus mocked him with feathered hatred from the skies. And that injured bird was hopping fearlessly towards him out of the corn!

He blasted it, reduced it to a heap of bloody feathers. *And now the sky was darkening as the winged hordes grew in numbers, circling above him like desert vultures waiting for their weakening prey to die.*

Another shot, not picking a target this time, just blasting upwards. The ranks did not even part, no bird fell. And that was when Gary Shank knew that he had to flee for his life.

He scrambled over the stile and began to run down the sloping field, hearing those crows screaming their hate at him. Louder and still louder, closer and closer, hundreds of them were swooping in low, circling to get ahead of him, barring his escape route.

He was frightened, more scared than he had been

that day in the release pen. Because crows were black and evil and there were so many more of them. He had witnessed how they fed on the corpses hanging from the vermin gibbet in the woodland clearing, pecking out the dead eyes first, then raking the flesh into ribbons, gouging it with their hooked beaks. Carnivores, feeding on the dead and the living, it mattered not which to them. Suddenly he had become the hunted, he was *food*!

He fired from the hip, this time cutting a path through the ranks which fluttered and cawed only twenty yards in front of him. His shot charge dropped three birds: two dead and one fluttering on its back, legs kicking. Another blast; one down this time, but it kept the big lot at bay. Crazed as they were, they feared for their lives.

He ran again, loading and firing as he went, once over his shoulder as half a dozen of them set their wings and glided at his unprotected back. Not stopping to fire, shooting on the run, his marksmanship was erratic. The belt of cartridges around his waist was becoming lighter all the time. And in the end sheer weight of numbers would win the day for the Corby crows.

He was crying, sobbing uncontrollably, wanting to be back at the kitchen table with a plate of rabbit stew in front of him; they always had rabbit for lunch on Saturdays, a kind of Shank tradition, summer or winter.

One bird, bolder than the rest, caught him unawares as he turned to shoot behind him, its stabbing beak ripping the cloth of his ex-army jacket. He shot at it as it departed. *And missed with his last cartridge*!

He reversed his hold on the gun and gripped it by the barrel, wielding it in the manner of a club. He stood at bay, for if he ran they would surely dive at his back and fell him. The black cloud no more than ten yards above his head seemed like a canopy of death about to smother him. A myriad of malevolent eyes gleamed amidst the flapping wings, beaks widened in anticipation of the flesh which they would strip from the bones, leaving the bloodied skeleton to dry in the scorching sun.

Swooping, diving – and then they were rising in a maelstrom of clamouring panic as a double blast of shot cut into their ranks. Five fell; their packed formation left no gaps for wasted shot. Another two fluttered down and flapped in terror on the sun-scorched grass. Milling, they fought one another to gain height and safety, but not fast enough to escape another devastating twin gunshot.

Gary was too dazed to understand. He only knew that his father was at his side, grasping him with a strong hand, using the double-barrelled shotgun pistol-fashion even though the frenzied crows were now out of range.

He was being dragged along, stumbling but somehow keeping his footing. He was still crying when they came in sight of the cottage and the crow noise was but a distant cacophony of thwarted evil. Crying with relief now because he would be eating rabbit stew after all.

10

Brian Barker had roamed parts of the Corby estate ever since his parents moved into the council houses at the far end of the village. He spent as much time away from home as possible, which pleased both himself and his parents; he didn't want to have to listen to their frequent quarrelling, it became boring day after day. Going fishing was a way of life for the freckled thirteen-year-old. Not that he ever caught much, and most of what he did he put back in the river. Except for trout. Mrs Winston in the bungalow on the main road would always buy a trout for 50p. He hoped his father wouldn't find out because he'd only confiscate the money and treat himself to an extra half down at the pub.

Brian hated his father. Tom Barker hadn't had a job for as long as the boy could remember and spent most of the day sleeping off the previous night's drinking. And he was always in a bad temper when he woke up. So Brian learned not to linger in the house after he came home from school; mostly his mother gave him money to buy some chips from the van which called at the village most evenings and he would go on from there down to the river. One good thing, his parents never scolded him for coming home late; in fact, he decided that they probably wouldn't miss him if he didn't return home at all. Not until next morning, anyway. They were often both drunk; quarrelled, sometimes came to blows, and Brian couldn't remember the last time they had looked into his room on their way up to bed.

He had tried to become friendly with Gary Shank, the keeper's son. Gary was in the same class at the comprehensive in Stratford and they travelled to and from school on the bus together. Previously Brian had sneaked down to the river and nobody had bothered him but it could be awkward now that there was a gamekeeper prowling about the Corby estate. And, anyway, it would be fun to know a gamekeeper. But it hadn't worked out quite like that.

'Fancy goin' fishin' tonight?' Brian had made sure he occupied the seat next to Gary.

'I'm too busy.' Gary looked out of the window and wished that somebody else had grabbed that spare seat. This kid was becoming a pest; and he smelled, too. A kind of unwashed odour combined with stale cooking smells.

'Doin' what?'

'Helping my dad. I'm the assistant gamekeeper now, and that's official.'

'Blimey!' Brian sniffed his admiration and drew the back of his hand across his nose. 'And you get *paid* for it?'

'I might do.' *Cheeky sod*.

'Well, *I'm* goin' fishin' tonight, anyway.'

'Where?'

'The river, of course. There's a good place just by the bend where it gets shallower. I 'ad a trout there last night, and a grayling two nights ago. Mrs Winston will buy – '

'You're not allowed to fish the river there. Nobody's allowed to fish any part of the river which runs through the estate.' Gary was annoyed.

'And who says so?'

'My dad, for a start. On Mr Broughton's orders. The fishing is being let.'

'Bugger 'em, they ain't stoppin' me, neither your dad nor Mr Broughton.'

'They'll get the police to you if they catch you.'

'They've gotta catch me first.' Brian stuck up two fingers and blew a raspberry. 'And I suppose you'll go and twit to your old man now I've told you.'

'I might mention it.' Gary turned away and continued looking out of the window. The sooner this boy stopped following him around, the better, Gary thought. He was becoming a nuisance. Gary hated anybody deliberately trying to make friends. He knew that if he didn't keep Brian at bay he'd start coming up to the cottage and become a regular pest.

'Bloody snob!' Brian raised his hand again, this time clenching his fist. 'You try and get me into trouble, mate, and you'll be spittin' out your fucking teeth. If I want to fish, I will. The land belongs to the people, nobody has a right to own *any* of it. My dad says so. See?'

Gary did not reply. It was a relief when the bus pulled up at the village stop and Brian Barker got off. Out of the corner of his eye Gary noticed those two fingers saluting the bus as it moved off again. He most certainly would mention it to his father.

Brian's father wasn't there when the boy walked into the house. He might still be in bed, although he was usually watching the television in the kitchen by four-thirty. Or he might have left home like he was always threatening to do. Good riddance if he had, Brian thought, but somehow that was too much to hope for.

'There's thirty pence on the dresser,' his mother said without looking up from the dog-eared paperback she was reading. 'Get yourself some chips and don't 'ang around makin' a bloody nuisance of yourself.'

Brian grabbed the money. The last thing he wanted was to hang around. He went outside, took his fishing rod out of the lean-to shed and set off back towards the village. Less than five minutes in the house, the way he liked it. And if that stuck-up little bugger or his dad tried to interfere with him. . . .

It was peaceful down by the river. Brian situated himself in his favourite place; worms were becoming harder to find each day, it was the dry weather that was making them burrow deeper, he reckoned. He baited his line, cast it out into the shallows and settled down to wait. He had a feeling that this was going to be his lucky night. Two trout, maybe, and a quid from Mrs Winston. She was a snooty bitch, wouldn't allow him over the doorstep like he had the bleedin' plague or something. Still, she always paid up and that was all that mattered. Two it was going to be tonight.

He must have been here an hour, and not so much as a nibble at his worm. When the river was low, like it was now, was always the best time to catch a trout. Not that there was any hurry, there were several hours left until darkness, but one in the bag early on would have been nice. Those crows in the wood were makin' a lot of noise, got on his bloody nerves after a while. No sign of Gary Shank nor his dad. No, they wouldn't trouble about a schoolkid tryin' for a fish, they'd better things to do. Not that it would make any difference. Stuck-up little bastard, thought he was somebody just because his old man was a gamekeeper. But not for long, there was talk in the village that some of them were gettin' up a petition to stop the shootin' on the estate. There were interferin' fuckers everywhere, somebody always tryin' to stop somebody else from doin' somethin' they liked doin'. He wished those bleedin' crows would give it a rest, just for five minutes.

And then the water rippled a yard or so out from the bank. Brian tensed. That was a trout for sure, seen the worm and comin' for it. He gripped the rod, waiting. *Come on, you little bugger, let's have you!*

Christ, it was a big 'un! He had a glimpse of it below the surface and craned his neck but it had passed into a clump of reeds. It had looked about two foot long, probably an underwater distortion of its size but nevertheless it was huge, far bigger than any he had caught before. It might be a record! He grinned at the thought; that would put the bloody Shanks in their place and no mistake!

Where the bloody hell was it? Disappointed because it had not reappeared, he resisted the urge to wind in his line and cast it nearer to those reeds. If it had seen the worm then it would either come or it wouldn't, there was no way he could make it. He was sweating, his hands slippery on the rod.

A shadow; he jerked his head round but again he was too late. The fish was close in to the bank, directly below him and screened from his view. It *must* have seen the bait, he decided. Any second now! He began to take the strain in readiness.

Minutes passed and still nothing happened. Perhaps the trout, *if* it was a trout, had swum on downstream close to the bank and was gone. He began to groan silently to himself and then he heard a splash, a parting of the water by some heavy body. Jeez, it might even be a salmon that had lost its direction and swum all the way up here from the sea.

And then the creature was perched on the bank less than a yard away, regarding him steadily. Boldly. Menacingly.

Brian had no idea what it was. A dark-coloured lithe body with a bushy tail, a head that seemed too small, eyes that blazed its ferocity, its lust. The creature tensed, dripping water. It wasn't far off his original estimation of its size, maybe eighteen inches. An otter? No, he didn't think so. More like a stoat but too big and the wrong colour. Jaws open, showing wicked-looking teeth, it was snarling at him.

He swallowed. He would have backed away if there was anywhere to go. There wasn't. But it wouldn't attack, wild creatures in this country didn't unless they were cornered. Did they? He wasn't sure, but he didn't care for the way it was eyeing him.

'Shoo!' It was almost a plea. 'Go on, fella, *shoo*!'

Its sudden leap was too fast for the eye to follow, a dark streak that glinted momentarily in the evening sunshine. Brian had no time to throw up an arm to ward the animal off, and his scream of terror was stifled as powerful fangs sank into his throat. Blinding pain. He almost passed out as he fell backwards, his fishing rod slipping from his grasp and plopping into the river. He grabbed the wriggling, clinging body, feeling the power that throbbed within it, but he only helped it to tear the tender flesh of his gashed neck. So strong, it was impossible to dislodge it, its sharp claws raking his chest, shredding his grubby shirt. Thick, warm sticky blood started to spout into the air, scintillating in the sunlight.

A frenzied man-eater from some far-off land – he panicked as his crazed brain ran riot – a mongoose from India that was capable of killing deadly snakes. It could not be anything else. His struggles were growing weaker, everywhere was going dark. He was giving up, surrendering. His feeble blood-drenched body was only twitching now as his life slipped away in a rivulet of crimson that soaked into the parched soil beneath him.

So intent was the carnivore on its feast of human flesh and blood that its habitual wariness was momentarily dulled. Gorging itself, it was tearing, slurping, raking with its claws as it ate. A snapping twig, then a shadow fell on it, and the creature looked up to see the shirt-sleeved man with gun raised, an expression of horror on his features.

One bound took the creature from its kill back on to the bank. Another would have plunged it to safety, but in that instant a lethal charge of buckshot ripped into it, rolling the near-severed elongated body into an unrecognizable mulch, a heap of dark furry bloody flesh that did not even twitch.

'Jesus God!' Gordon Shank lowered his smoking shotgun and stood between his son and the carnage which confronted them. 'A bloody *mink*!'

Men and dogs were assembled on the river bank. Yapping hounds fretted to surge forward and find a scent but were restrained by their training and the small man in drill trousers and wellington boots whose word was their command. He cracked his whip and they fell back, whining impatiently.

'They'll follow mink from here to where the river ends.' Ron Ferris turned to John Broughton. 'And they won't leave a scent until I tell 'em.'

'I want every mink on this stretch of the river exterminated.' Broughton was visibly angry, a hunter whose bloodlust transcended his sporting instincts. 'This is what happens when these animal rights lunatics liberate mink. The creatures turn feral, kill anything and everything they can.' *Including humans.* 'We have to wipe 'em out, Mr Ferris, every last one of them, for the safety of the whole neighbourhood.' And the trout, he thought, because there won't be a fish left between here and Stratford unless we do and Vogt's man is coming on Monday. 'We're ready when you are.'

Ferris glanced around him, hearing the metallic snap of shotgun breeches being closed – Broughton, Shank, three plainclothes policemen with pump-action guns. He disapproved of the armoury – only he was unarmed – they didn't need guns, the hounds would kill the mink without any help once they got on the scent. For him, it was just another hunt. He had not seen the boy's mangled body, had only heard about it, and didn't really believe that a mink was the culprit because that was impossible. More likely the kid had been murdered by some perverted maniac and the animal had come upon the corpse and just investigated it; it wouldn't touch flesh that it had not killed itself. A scapegoat. He shrugged; it didn't really matter, it was good training for the dogs and they'd got precious little work since otter hunting was legally banned. 'Right, let's go.'

The six hounds rushed forward and plunged into the shallows, splashing, sniffing the edge of the bank, investigating a fringe of rushes. Moving as a pack, the big one, their leader, they worked methodically, silently; they would only give voice when they found scent.

Going downriver, swimming where it was deep enough but mostly working the banks, they went back and forth, in and out of the water. The men with guns tried to keep level with them but had to cut inland and make detours where the undergrowth on the side of the river was too dense. Ahead of them was Ferris, somehow keeping up with his hounds, whip coiled in his hand, urging them on. But they needed no directions for they knew their trade. And suddenly the big dog bayed, a deep-throated sound that cut menacingly through the balmy atmosphere of a summer evening.

'He's on to one,' Ferris called back, and broke into a run. 'Caesar's found one!'

The mink had been skulking beneath some leafy overhanging branches against the bank. As one, the pack turned at their leader's cry. Something dived into the water and was lost to view. *And then it was as though the whole river foamed, became a seething, boiling cauldron, the spray hiding the bloody scene from the watchers of the bank above.*

The baying turned to canine yelps of terror, cries of pain. Heavy bodies threshed, then were dragged below the surface, the sluggish current now resembling a surging tidal wave that crashed against the banks. Ferris was yelling but his words were drowned in the turmoil, just as his hounds were being dragged down and drowned by a dozen or more frenzied feral mink. Blood was staining the water pink, a dog was floating lifelessly with its attacker using it as a raft and savaging it as the swell buffeted it towards the side. The mink hounds were fleeing, the hunters had suddenly become the hunted. Large stoat-like bodies clung to their prey, biting savagely, awash in jugular blood.

The blast of a shotgun split the mayhem. The mink upon the floating dog jerked and slid back into the water. A volley from the police marksmen, and two more of the blood-lusting carnivores died, a hound yelping because some stray pellets had sprayed it.

'Mind the hounds!' Ferris was waving his whip frantically, aghast at the scene because it was a huntsman's nightmare, one from which he would surely awake at any second to hear his beloved hounds barking in their kennels beneath his bedroom window. He closed his eyes. Opening them again he saw a couple of mink dragging a shrieking dog back down the bank. Caesar was gone, drifting with the current. Three more were lying dead in the shallows. Igor was badly wounded, blood pouring from a gash in his neck; he had made it up on to dry land but he was certainly dying. Tiny heads were visible as mink swam to and fro in search of their prey. Another salvo of shots, the charges cutting up the surface in a cloud of vicious spray. The men were firing and firing again. Bodies large and small lay everywhere, a logjam of corpses was building up fifty yards downstream where the river narrowed and the undergrowth was thickest.

Finally there was just the awful silence, the atmosphere thick with gunsmoke. Grim-faced men lined the bank, staring in disbelief. Ferris was weeping openly for his hounds, Gordon Shank was seeing again that savaged youthful corpse with the mink feeding on it and knowing that it had been true. Three policemen were already mentally writing their reports and wondering if they would be believed. And John Broughton was thinking about Monday and the pending visit of Vogt's field master, and wondering if there might still be a trout left in the river.

'I think we got the lot.' Broughton voiced his hopes and tried to sound confident.

Gordon nodded. In all probability they had accounted for all the feral mink on this stretch of the Corby river; a bloody slaughter and a terrible price to pay in canine lives. Revenge for the Barker boy, that was what it had really been. Lives for a life. Apart from that, they had not achieved anything. One species on the estate had been exterminated. Hopefully. But it wasn't just the mink, it was every form of wildlife which abounded in these fields and woods that threatened any who ventured there. The Corby Curse was far-reaching, and this was only the beginning.

11

Pamela had spent most of that afternoon trying to put everything into perspective. For a start, she could find no logical reason why she was still here in Corby House.

The damaged Justy had been towed to a garage in Stratford. The insurance company's assessor would come and look at it within the next few days and hopefully sanction the necessary work. The car might be off the road for a fortnight. But that was no problem; she could easily have hired another. Or called a taxi to take her to the station and got the InterCity back to London, back to safety and the social life she loved. But she had not done any of those things. Why?

Certainly not because of her husband, nor because she had a new home in the prestigious Heart of England. A kind of procrastination, she decided; never do today what you can do tomorrow. She had been like that right from her schooldays. Even tomorrow she might not leave. She had had the opportunity to go down to London with John the other day and had turned it down. Maybe because he had presumed she would accompany him and she was being deliberately stubborn. Now, instead of taking dainty afternoon tea with a social equal in a plush Mayfair suite, she was drinking out of a mug and eating home-made cake in a gamekeeper's kitchen. A few weeks ago she would have cringed at the idea of mixing below her own status; now it did not seem to matter. In some ways it was almost a relief. She gave up trying to analyse herself because there was no pattern to her behaviour.

Yesterday's newspaper lay on the table. Its bold front page headline had a hypnotic effect on her: MAN-EATING MINK: THE CORBY CURSE? She had not read the leading article, had no wish to.

'This German feller's due tomorrow.' Jill Shank was busying herself preparing a casserole for their evening meal. 'Gordon's gone to the fish farm in Wales to fetch a few hundred trout. They've put mesh barriers at both ends off the river on the Corby boundaries to keep 'em in. So at least the bloke will see some trout.'

'I know.' Pamela yawned. 'John's been panicking about it. But I think he's got his priorities wrong. A boy was savaged to death but all John thinks about is whether the trout will be all right. Me, I'm worried about what's going to happen next.'

'Me, too.' Jill came back to the table, a worried expression on her face. 'School holidays start next week and I'm sending Claire to spend a fortnight with my parents. At least I know she'll be safe there. I wish Gary could go too, but he won't. I'm scared every time he goes up to the woods even if he does have his gun with him. If it hadn't been for Gordon last week there's no knowing what those crows would have done to him. It's crazy, the way they massed and tried to mob him. But Gordon's sorted 'em out.' She laughed but it lacked conviction. 'He went out before daybreak, put a dead sheep in the field and put some alpha chloralose in it. The devils were lying all over the place. Some managed to fly back to the wood and dropped there. He and Gary picked up *hundreds*!'

'A life for a life.' Pamela shook her head. 'Revenge, that's all it amounts to. The mink kill a boy, so we kill a dozen of them. Crows attack your son, so hundreds of them have to die for it. But how many more lives are going to be lost? Tell me.' She hesitated and seemed embarrassed. 'Do you . . . do you think there's anything in this Corby legend?'

'I dunno.' Jill was staring at the newspaper now. 'I've never believed in that sort of thing. At least, not until now. But I reckon there has to be more to it. Okay, the animals are acting out of character, going crazy, but there could be other factors responsible. Chemicals on the land, radioactive fallout . . . who knows?'

'But it's only happening *here*, on this estate.' Pamela still bore the strain of her traumatic experience the other night. 'Fifty yards over the boundaries, on neighbouring land, everything's perfectly normal. John has checked with the adjoining farmers to find out what sprays, insecticides, herbicides they're using, but they're using exactly the same as our own tenant farmers. So that rules that out. And when you've eliminated everything else it all comes back to the Corby Curse. Unbelievable, but it's happening. The forerunner of these animal liberationists decreed that no animal should be killed on Corby lands, and because he was defied a couple of hundred years later we have to pay the price. Oh, God, I wish John would give in, sell up before it's too late!'

'It's too late now.' Jill was staring out of the window. 'The sanctuary clause has been deleted from the deeds. Shooting and fishing are in demand, at a premium. Somebody else would buy the estate for the same reason as your husband. The killing won't stop, either by sportsmen or animals. The media love it; there was brief coverage on the national news on television last night. Gordon says that the next thing will be these crazy animal libbers turning up to take sides with the animals. And when that happens the Corby lands will become a battleground.'

'Maybe I'll go back to London.' Pamela finished her drink and scraped her chair back. But she knew she wouldn't because she felt a kind of compulsion to remain – because of her new friendship with a working-class girl. Which was as crazy as everything that had happened to her so far. High society had become distasteful all of a sudden, and that realisation astounded her.

Karl Rubisch was tall, with thick fair hair and an angular face that seemed to droop, and reminded John Broughton of a disconsolate bloodhound. Sharp-eyed, noting everything that went on around him on the drive back from Birmingham airport, he was a man of few words, possibly because his knowledge of the English language was scanty. After a while John gave up trying to make conversation. It was as though the German resented it because it taxed his limited vocabulary.

Mrs Arkwright served dinner in the dining room of Corby House, a solemn affair in view of the language difficulty. Pamela found it a bore but her upbringing had taught her to be the perfect hostess. John served the wine, noting that rich claret was the German's weakness; ply him with enough and he would either talk or fall asleep, he thought. Anything was preferable to those long spells during which nobody spoke, just fidgeted with their cutlery in between courses.

'There are plenty of trout in the river.' John finally broached the subject of the fishing, which seemed to have been deliberately avoided up until now.

'Ah, that is so good but tomorrow I will see them for myself with my own eyes.' Rubisch tapped his rimless spectacles but no smile stretched his lips. 'And the mink?' Head forward, he stared almost belligerently at his host.

'Oh, yes, the mink.' Broughton took a sip of wine. 'Yes, well, we shot the lot. There was no harm done.'

'Except the dogs. And ... the boy. *Mein Gott!*'

'It was unfortunate. Tragic. But I assure you there are no mink left in this stretch of river.'

A long silence and then, 'But the ... other animals?'

'No problem, really. A chap got stung by a swarm of bees, but that has happened many times in the past elsewhere. A woman trod on a snake and got bitten. The newspapers exaggerated, blew it all up out of proportion.'

Pamela felt her skin prickling. There was an icy chill creeping up her back. God, she would never forget the other night. But her husband wanted to sweep all that under the carpet.

'Herr Vogt is worried.' Those baleful eyes did not blink, the features were static. 'For him I must check. Everything. Everywhere.'

'Oh, yes. Of course. No problem.' Pamela could see that her husband was shaken. Rubisch was here to look the whole place over. Not just the river. He would see the pheasants going crazy in the release pens. Hear the night sounds ...

'Tomorrow I shall see for myself.' He tapped his glasses again; he might have been smirking but it was impossible to tell. Vogt's troubleshooter, and he was looking for trouble.

Pamela awoke sometime during the early hours. She had been in the habit of doing so most nights, as if an alarm clock had been set by the bedside. She tried not to listen to the rustling of birds in the bushes below, the soft fluttering of moth wings against the window pane, the thump of a bat . . . the gathering force of evil outside. That was when the nightmare drive came back to her: the stag wrenching the radiator grill apart with its wicked antlers, the badger's bones cracking and crunching as she drove over it, the wounded creature following her all the way down to the keeper's cottage, still trying to get to her. Tensing, almost writhing in the bed beside her soundly sleeping husband, she wanted to scream aloud, to wake him so that he could listen, too.

And then the howling began. It seemed to come from somewhere up towards the home covert, reverberating in the still night air. At first it was a yapping, the barking of dog foxes answered by the eerie screams of vixens, a vulpine chorus. Now it was different: long-drawn-out howls, mournful to begin with but becoming more angry, almost a roaring. Other creatures took it up until it came from all directions, a sound that vibrated her body. Vengeful, lusting, the cry of carnivores demanding fresh meat. Human meat!

Which was stupid, she tried to tell herself. It was foxes, that was all. Okay, they were vicious creatures but they couldn't do her any harm. Not out there, anyway. Just noisy. Shank was killing them almost daily; seldom a morning went by when there was not one caught in a snare, but still they howled the night away. So loud, so insistent.

But John slept through it all and she hated him for

it. The selfish bastard, he was trying to convince Vogt that everything was fine here, but this fellow Rubisch would find out all right. He was shrewd, he didn't miss a trick. Lives were being put at risk for the sake of sport – for money.

Tonight was the noisiest she had ever known, a bestial chorus of savagery. She felt the sheer hatred, their insatiable lust for human meat. A few days ago she would have attempted to dismiss it as fanciful fears, but not after those mink in the river. A boy had been partially eaten. The foxes would do the same if they could get at her. But they couldn't because the doors were locked. They couldn't get in.

She tensed because she heard another noise. Close; only yards away. A kind of soft shuffling that creaked old floorboards. Oh, God, *no*! Her hand was reaching out to shake her slumbering husband awake when she realized, recognized that familiar, almost apologetic habitual cough with which the German punctuated his long periods of silence. She let out her breath in audible relief. Karl Rubisch was awake, perhaps on his way to the toilet. She waited to hear the cistern flush but there was no rush of water. Nothing. Perhaps he had gone back to bed. Shortly before dawn the animal noises died away and Pamela drifted back into an uneasy sleep.

Karl Rubisch was downstairs in the dining room when Pamela entered. He nodded and gave that cough again, for which she was grateful. Yes, it had been him on the landing last night. She'd needed confirmation for her own peace of mind.

He wore a thornproof jacket over his shirt, plus twos that were tucked into his long stockings, and polished leather boots – a huntsman risen early. She refrained from asking him if he had slept well.

'I'll make some coffee.' She tried to smile. 'There are rolls and jam on the table, cereal if you would like it. Please help yourself. Mrs Arkwright doesn't arrive until nine.' She was automatically apologising for the absence of servants; apologising for everything.

'Tell me.' He struggled to find the right words. 'In England, do they still have . . . the *wolves*?'

'Wolves!'

'*Ja*! For them I heard in the night. They howled in the forest just as they do in my homeland. Or perhaps there is a . . . what do you call it . . . a menagerie close by?'

'I . . . I really don't know.' She felt those icy fingers stroking their way up her spine again. 'No, not wolves, Herr Rubisch. Only in zoos. I think perhaps you heard foxes last night.'

'The fox is the cousin of the wolf.' He shrugged his shoulders. 'The difference is small. Perhaps I am mistaken.'

'Good morning, Herr Rubisch.' John Broughton strode into the room. 'Again it looks like being a wonderful day. Let's breakfast, and then my gamekeeper and I will take you down to the river.'

'And to the other places,' the German added meaningfully. 'I shall be truly interested to see what the Corby estate has to offer our clients from home.'

The river meadows were a mass of bright yellow buttercups in the serene English summer morning as Broughton and Karl Rubisch followed in the gamekeeper's footsteps. Shank was wearing his shooting suit of cord breeches and jacket to match, on his employer's instructions. Today everything had to be formal; their humourless visitor would not be impressed by casual wear. Shank was tense, glancing about him. But nothing seemed amiss.

'Look at those down there.' Shank pointed into the shallows where the early morning sun showed clearly a school of trout amidst the vegetation – fully grown fish straight from the farm in Powys still exploring their new surroundings.

'See.' There was no mistaking the relief in Broughton's tone. 'I told you the mink had not done any harm.'

Trout and more trout. Broughton's relief merged into euphoria. They went on, past the place where Brian Barker had died, up as far as where the watercourse narrowed, the scene of that bloody battle a few days ago, then back downstream. Still more trout darted, to and fro in the sunlit shallows.

'Superb fishing,' Broughton commented. 'One of the best rivers in England.'

'I now would like to view the rest.' The German was emotionless, expressionless. He had seen the fish but there was no way of telling if he was satisfied.

'Oh, yes, fine.' Broughton nodded. 'Maybe you would like to see the pheasants now in the release pens. Really superb birds, bred from a truly wild strain. But you will see for yourself.'

Shank led the way back across the sloping meadow. He felt almost undressed without a gun under his arm. These last few weeks he had taken to carrying it wherever he went. But today he could not. Everything must appear normal; gamekeepers did not go to armed on tours of inspection for foreign sporting agencies.

Yates had turned his cattle into the river meadows, Shank noted as they topped the brow of a small hillock. Charolais heifers, about a dozen of them grazing the long grass. That was fine.

'The foxes make noises in the night.' Rubisch broke the long silence. 'That is strange at this time of year when mostly the vixens are busy with their cubs and the males lie in cover. It is not the mating season. They sounded . . . *disturbed*!'

'We're getting them down.' Broughton spoke quickly, perhaps too quickly to be convincing. 'Shank here is killing a lot. The trouble is that there has never been any vermin control until this year and –'

A loud mooing interrupted him, making him look up. Those cattle had moved surprising quickly and were now bunched on the slope just behind the trio. Heads up, they were watching the humans, tails swishing to and fro. And there was no mistaking the mood of bovine anger in their posture.

Broughton was aware that he was sweating and his legs seemed suddenly weak. Glancing round, he mentally calculated how far it was to the gate. Thirty-five, forty yards. Charolais were of uncertain temperament; sometimes deceptively quiet, other times frisky, even nasty, like bulls – vicious. Now they were starting to paw the ground, snorting.

They either ignored or resented human presence. And at this moment they seemed decidedly unfriendly. Broughton wished that Gordon Shank would quicken his step; their visitor had stopped, blissfully unaware of the restless cattle, to watch a hovering kestrel. *For Christ's sake don't hang about*!

'I think –'

Whatever Karl Rubisch thought the others were not destined to hear, for at that moment the parched meadowland beneath their feet began to vibrate with a rapid drumming sound that became louder and louder, like the beginnings of an earthquake deep in the bowels of the earth forcing its way upwards.

'*Run*!' John Broughton leaped forward, aware that Gordon Shank was ahead of him, and presumed that Rubisch, too, was sprinting with them. It was only when he looked back that he became aware that the German field master had not moved but stayed where he was, rooted to the ground in sheer terror. 'Oh, Jesus, the bloody fool!'

The cattle were stampeding down the incline, heads lowered, their size belying their speed, thundering, snorting. They were hornless but their solid heads were terrifying battering rams as they singled out one who had stayed behind, the others forgotten.

Broughton didn't want to watch but he could not drag his eyes away. Helpless, a mere spectator, he did not even shout because it would have been futile. Instinctively clutching at his companion, he was praying for a miracle which would not happen. Because there was no escape for the German.

The leading heifer caught Rubisch and threw him into the air. Even amidst the noise of the onrushing beasts the two men heard bones snap. The body splayed as it was tossed, its posture a blasphemous crucifixion. Folding, falling, it was lost under a forest of pounding hooves. The flattened bloody mulch stained the buttercups crimson in the wake of the trampling herd.

For one awful moment John Broughton thought that the Charolais would rush on towards himself and the gamekeeper. But they were wheeling, seemingly oblivious of the other humans, and swinging back towards their victim, slowing momentarily then gathering speed again; and charging. Another crazed stampede, and then they slowed, trotted back and stood looking down on the remnants of Karl Rubisch, a kind of unholy animal satisfaction in their stance. For a minute, perhaps two, they savoured their mutilation, then those bloody hooves began to paw, crushing and ripping, tearing the corpse apart, sniffing at it. *Licking it with their rough tongues.*

Broughton was aware of his companion backing away and followed him. They were at the gate, struggling to unlatch it, then going through and closing it after them. And leaning on it because they had not the strength to walk any further. Trying not to vomit as the bile scorched their throats, they watched that huddle of cattle, seeing them walk unconcernedly away and start grazing again.

There was silence, except for the buzzing of the flies which swarmed and fed on that human morass spread amongst the buttercups.

12

Lucy Titley made a remarkable recovery from her snakebite in spite of her age. She spent a week in hospital. The swelling went down and left her with a stiffness; she could have been sent home on the third day but the doctors advised her to remain due to the fact that she lived alone and there was nobody to look after her. She agreed with some reluctance. Her only worry was for the animals on the Corby estate. The antibloodsport people had promised her their support but were they really going to do anything? What about all those poor pheasants penned up and waiting to be shot? Had the donkey's feet been trimmed? Well, she would find out the moment she was mobile again.

Lucy was a woman of extremes. Her whole life was devoted to the welfare of animals but she loathed humans. Humans, with the exception of a very few, were responsible for all the cruelty to poor dumb creatures. Especially children. Little bastards! She hated them, especially the modern generation: uncouth, undisciplined, vandals and thieves! They threw litter into her front garden deliberately and once a stone had broken a window. They recognized her as a threat to their useless existence. She phoned the police innumerable times but they did nothing except promise to look into the matter. That Barker boy had got what he deserved and she had no pity for him, nor his layabout good-for-nothing parents in their supposed grief. The boy had gone down to the river deliberately to inflict cruelty, hooking fish out of the water to die a painful, lingering death. That mink was only protecting the inhabitants of the water. She felt sorry for the dogs; it wasn't their fault, their sadistic owners were to blame for encouraging them to hunt down harmless creatures of the wild.

It was fully time that she was back on the estate supervising things.

She bore no malice towards the adder which had attacked her, and was thankful it had escaped. She was convinced it hadn't been the snake's fault that it bit her. She was convinced the species had been unjustifiably persecuted for so long that they understandably regarded people as enemies. During the few days in which she was compelled to remain inactive her temper worsened, her sullen brooding needed only the slightest provocation to spark off an uncontrollable rage. Rages did her no good. Dr Westbury had warned her that if she allowed herself to get out of control she might have a heart attack or a stroke. But she had survived a lifetime of tantrums and rages so they really weren't going to do her a lot of harm now, she decided, and if they did then she had had a good life. Her small savings were willed to the RSPCA and they would carry on where she had left off, she was fully confident of that. Her diary and notebook were lodged with her solicitor, the closely written pages listing the names of all those who perpetrated cruelty towards animals in the village, and she hoped that those who followed her would see that justice was done. The police were a waste of time, and the last officer who had called to see her regarding a complaint she had made about the Jones children had been positively rude. She ought to have reported him to his superiors but it was too late now.

Today she felt much better, so she would go back to the Corby estate for her usual walk down the long track from the main road, check on Major, then go past that awful gamekeeper's cottage and up to the big wood. Corby Wood, *not* the home covert as these bloodsports people had renamed it. She went into the kitchen and rummaged in the tool cupboard until she found the small hacksaw which she kept there for cutting up bones for the neighbouring dogs; she wondered if it was strong enough to saw through the padlock on the door of the pheasant prison. Most certainly she would give it a try. She donned a pair of old cord trousers, struggled into her wellington boots (just in case she met another adder, poor persecuted dears) and let herself out of the bungalow.

There were some children hanging about further up the road. She squinted in the brightness of the sunlight and recognized the two Jones boys. Her lips tightened, her knuckles clenched. The little bastards, they were sure to be up to no good. She would have shouted after them had not they moved away, running on ahead of her. She saw two other boys come out of a driveway and join them. She was almost certain those were the Morris brothers, who came from a respectable family that went to church every Sunday. Now what on earth were they doing mixing with the Joneses? Lucy thought about calling in and telling their parents but there wasn't time, she had a long walk ahead of her. Maybe she would on the way back.

Half a mile further on she saw the track that led down from the main road on the once sacred Corby lands. She pursed her lips and anger coursed through her ageing body so that her pulses pounded; those boys, all four of them, they were going on to the estate, too!

'Hey!' she shouted, but knew that her words were drowned by the roar of passing traffic. 'You've no business going to the woods!'

If they heard her, they ignored her, and minutes later they were lost to her view down the winding cart track. She increased her pace until she became breathless and had to stop for a moment. The Joneses and the Morisses were bent on destruction of some kind, there was no doubt about that. Wherever the Joneses went there was always trouble and now they were leading those usually nice Morris lads astray, corrupting them; perhaps taking them birds'-nesting or catapulting. She would see to it that they were stopped from using the entrance to the Corby estate; the fact that it was a public right of way made no difference. She would inform Mr and Mrs Morris, and if the parents did not do anything about it then she would report them to the police. And that young officer had better show some respect for her this time.

Her heart was beating fast and temper gave her the strength to walk quickly again. But she did not catch up with those boys. They knew they were guilty and had run, she concluded, probably cut back home across the fields. A loud braying made her jump. There was Major looking at her through a gap in the hedge, lips drawn back to expose strong teeth in a kind of donkey leer. He did not look friendly and she recalled their last meeting.

'I've brought something for you, Major.' She pulled a carrot from her pocket and decided to throw it into the field rather than risk him biting her fingers. *They* had made him like that; he always used to be docile before those Broughton people took over and began ill-treating him so that he now mistrusted everybody. The carrot landed somewhere in the grass on the other side of the hedge; she heard the animal looking for it, then came a crunching of strong teeth. Good, the donkey had found it, now she had better have a peep at those feet. She tried to part the hawthorn without spiking herself, but it was too thick for her to be able to see more than an outline of Major. No, it would be too risky to go back to the stile and clamber over. She would look again on the way back and perhaps be afforded a clearer view.

The gamekeeper's cottage came into sight, a wisp of smoke curling from the chimney. Her anger returned. She was almost too breathless to shout but she would do her best. Never mind that the ogre's wife had taken her in that day and they had driven her to hospital. That in no way atoned for their disgraceful behaviour towards God's creatures. They had only done it to try to sweet-talk her into abandoning her constant war against their way of life. In fact, secretly they probably hoped that she would die from the viper's venom.

'Murderers!' she yelled, knowing that it was no more than an out-of-breath croak. 'Murderers, the lot of you!'

There was no movement from within the cottage, but Lucy knew that the occupants were there all right because the Land Rover was parked outside and the front door was open. They were hiding from her, hoping that she would believe they were out.

'Cowards!' It was all that she could do to get the words out. 'You can hide from me but it won't do you any good!'

She felt a little faint. It was the heat, of course. The weathermen had said only last night that this was the hottest summer since 1976. But if she fainted she didn't want the Shanks taking her in and reviving her. She would rather lie out here and die! No way was she accepting favours from the likes of *them*!

It took her a long time to reach the big wood. The path was steep and winding and she had to rest every few yards. She felt slightly sick. There was no hurry, she told herself, she had all day. Yes, there was an urgency, for every minute she delayed, those poor birds were suffering the ignominy and terror of being caged up.

Suddenly she heard voices, laughing, shouting; somebody swore in a juvenile voice. Lucy stopped to listen, holding on to a silver birch sapling to steady herself.

'Here, Barry you 'ave a go. See if you can 'it that fucking blackbird. Use your eyes, 'e's up there, top of that tree!'

The Joneses without a doubt! Lucy heard a loud *twang*, the rush of a missile hurtling up into the leafy foliage.

'You've missed the fucker. I knew you would. Now 'e's flown off. 'Ang on, let's look for another.'

They were catapulting, as she had feared, trying to

kill innocent *protected* birds! Well, she would have the law on them, but first she would have words. And, she decided, as she forced herself to hurry forward, she was going to fence this path off. She would do it herself, take some of those rotting stakes from the woodcutter's pile she had passed further back and block the way with them. Later. First, she had to stop this needless slaughter. She rounded a bend and saw the four boys clustered together some fifteen yards ahead, two of them picking up round stones for ammunition for their weapon.

'You ignorant little bastards!' she shrieked, waving her arms as she ran forward. 'Bastards! I'm going to give you a bloody good hiding!'

They looked up, stared, then started to run. She gained some satisfaction from the fact that they were afraid of her but she would rather have caught them and pummelled her bony fists into their faces, seeing their noses streaming with scarlet blood and hearing their cries of pain and guilt. She stopped and had to fight for her breath. All right, you're as cowardly as that gamekeeper and his family, she thought, the same disgusting breed. I won't even tell your parents, I'll ring the police direct when I get home. I know you shot at me with that catapult, don't you lie and deny it. *And* you called me a shit, I heard you. The Joneses, not the Morrises. The Morrises were foolish enough to accompany the others. Let's hope I'm in time to stop them being corrupted, because Mrs Morris usually does my shopping for me when she goes to town in snowy weather. Mrs Morris will probably thank me for reporting those abominable Jones children.

She knew she wasn't going to catch them now. She had to rest, seating herself down on a grassy bank. I'll be all right in a minute or two, she told herself. It was so very warm, she felt quite sleepy. Her eyelids wanted to droop so she let them.

She awoke with a start. The sun was low in the

western sky but it could not possibly be evening yet. No, she was mistaken and had lost her sense of where the points of the compass lay. It could not be more than two o'clock at the latest. She stood up, feeling refreshed after her brief rest; it wasn't far up to the pheasant pen now. Those magnificent birds would soon be free to roam the woods as they pleased. She felt in her handbag and slid out the hacksaw.

She heard the pheasants before she came upon the pen. The cock birds were shouting angrily for their freedom, protesting against man's cruelty; the hens were clucking almost like domestic fowls. There was a constant passage of feet, round and round the inside perimeter, pacing just like caged beasts at the zoo.

They saw her and hissed, a carpet of near-featherless bleeding birds. God, what had that keeper been doing to them? Lucy seethed with a renewed anger. He had been beating them, probably borrowing the foxhunting man's whip to lash his feathered charges. The bastard, she would be calling at the cottage on her way back!

With a rush of wings and a thudding of airborne bodies they hurled themselves at the mesh surrounds of the pen, then dropped down to the ground. Crazy to escape. Fluttering, panicking, heads against the wire-netting, they hissed at Lucy.

She held the padlock with one hand and tried sawing at the clasp with the serrated blade. Damn, it was awkward to get at and it would not twist round to a more convenient position. Sawing until both hands ached, she was scratching the shiny steel but not making any impression upon it. She had to rest again. Dozens of pairs of tiny eyes were staring balefully at her in the gathering darkness.

Only now was she aware that it was dusk. The realisation came as a shock; then she must have slept longer than she had thought. Twilight, and there was no way she was going to free these birds tonight. She must return home, temporarily. She'd ring the police and report the Jones boys for shooting at her with their catapult and calling her a shit. Mind that you point out that the Morrises were in no way involved in either the assault or the foul language, she told herself. Then telephone the RSPCA and inform them that Mr Shank, the gamekeeper, has been beating his penned pheasants. They would surely come and set them free, and take the injured ones away for treatment at the vet's. Lucy would come back here tomorrow night just to make sure that her report had not been ignored. If it had, she would telephone her MP. And she was also going to hammer those stakes in across the path to make sure that none of the villagers came up here with their dogs to chase the rabbits and pheasants. She had noticed some dog muck earlier, and it was an offence to foul a footpath. She would tell the police about that, too.

She was trembling. She was aware how fast her heart was beating and that there was a roaring in her ears like a distant waterfall. She was tired; the effort had been a great strain upon her. Home now, she resolved, shout at the gamekeeper as she passed his house, make those phone calls even though it was getting late, and –

Something howled in the bushes just behind her. The growl rose in a crescendo and was taken up all around. Stealthy heavy movements, the rustling of foliage, the snapping of dry twigs, the chorus of bestial cries were terrifying in the deepening twilight of the wood.

She turned and pressed herself back against the wire mesh. A sharp beak stabbed her leg, bringing a gasp of pain to her lips. The pheasants were massing, pecking, trying to get at her. And ahead of her she saw huge canine-like shapes with pointed ears and bushy tails slinking out of the undergrowth. Four, maybe five of them were coming towards her, growling, snarling. Their eyes shone redly in the dim light, their slavering jaws gaped.

They stopped, crouched and watched her; waiting to

hear her scream before they sprang, carnivores of the night lusting for human flesh. Tearing out the scrawny throat, ripping her clothing in their hunger for her wrinkled meat, they fought one another for her.

And then feasted noisily on their kill.

13

The Corby village hall was packed for the protest meeting. All fire regulations were being ignored – people were standing in the aisles between the rows of chairs and even the porch outside was crowded. Not since the celebrations for the last royal wedding had the community gathered together in such numbers.

Rotund and fresh-faced, the Reverend Middlemoor had presumed his right to chair the meeting, the hostility of his parishioners towards him temporarily forgotten. Gone were the days when Corby boasted its own vicar and three services every Sunday; nowadays it was family communion twice a month. The dwindling congregation had temporarily returned to the fold in order to fight against the visiting clergyman's proposal to close the church and encourage what remained of his faithful flock to attend the mother church. The outcry had finally been heard by the theological hierarchy, resulting in a compromise. Middlemoor was apparently unruffled by his superiors' climbdown. Now he and the villagers were united in a common cause – to stop the killing of animals on the former sanctuary which was their legacy.

The meeting had begun with a minute's silence during which they remembered Brian Barker and Lucy Titley, tragic victims of this extraordinary but understandable rebellion by God's creatures. Middlemoor affected a pious expression, checked his wristwatch surreptitiously and cleared his throat. He rustled papers on the table before him and a sheaf was passed down to the front row of his audience – letters that required signatures. They would be sent *en bloc* to Westminster in the hope that Parliament would intervene. A difficult one this, an attempt to convince their elected representative in the House that the recent deaths were a direct result of the breaking of a pledge with Nature.

'This whole business has been most distressing over the past few months.' Middlemoor's smile vanished to be replaced by another expression of solemnity. 'We can only hope that there is a chance that the sanctuary status of the Corby estate will be restored. Maybe an appeal to the House of Lords will be successful, who knows? We can rest content in the knowledge that we have done everything humanly possible to bring back the peace and tranquillity to these lands which are truly our rightful heritage.'

'What about the Curse, vicar?' A voice asked from the rear of the hall.

Middlemoor hesitated, fidgeted with the waistband of his customary grey flannel trousers and cleared his throat again, stalling. An admission of such a phenomenon would border on the blasphemous, might earn him bad press, which would in due turn result in a reprimand from the bishop. 'I ... er, think we have to be ... realistic. We are not concerning ourselves with ... um ... *black magic*, rather the breaking of a centuries-old covenant. Let us fight on one issue, not confuse those who might be able to help us.'

'Poppycock!' Jim Wilson shouted. 'Folks have been attacked, killed. You know as well as we do what it's all about, vicar. What about an exorcism?'

There was a mixture of angry murmurs and sniggers. People were glancing uneasily at one another. Nobody cared much for Wilson, and even less for the clergyman, but they knew that what Wilson said was true. There was an animal revolt all around them, it wasn't safe to walk the estate any longer. Middlemoor was trying to fudge it, talking down to them just like he did in church, the hypocritical old bastard.

'I would urge every one of you' – he was speaking slowly, embarrassed now – 'to keep clear of the land in question until we have sorted something out through the proper channels.' The vicar's gaze alighted on a dark-haired young man seated three rows back from the stage, then switched to the attractive fair-haired girl beside him who wore a soiled hessian dress that failed to hide her bare feet, in a mute warning to his own son and his hippy girlfriend: *Don't take the law into your own hands*!

Glenn Middlemoor returned his father's admonishing look and squeezed Angela's hand as though to reassure her. The silly old bastard's not going to stop *us* doing what we know is right, he thought. No more than he managed to prevent us organizing a demonstration against the hunt last winter, even if it did result in us being bound over. He doesn't cut any ice with me; I might be his son but I'm not one of his bloody subservient parishioners.

Glenn and Angela had hitchhiked up from Wiltshire after the police roadblocks had prevented them reaching Stonehenge, along with the rest of the peace convoy. News had reached them of the happenings in the Heart of England and they saw another chance to strike a blow for animal rights. The clash with the hunt had been a disaster; now was their chance to take revenge. And lodging in the vicarage gave it an added touch of subtlety.

Glenn was glad that Lucy Titley was dead. On his last visit home, that occasion when he shocked his parents by bringing Angela with him, he took her down on to the estate. Despite a blazing row at the vicarage the previous evening, the couple had been compelled to sleep in different rooms. 'If you are bent on sinning,' his flushed father had shouted in a high-pitched voice, 'then it shall not be under *my* roof!' Which was why they went into the woods the following afternoon. Glenn was both angry and aroused.

There wouldn't be anybody about on a weekday afternoon, they were certain of that, so on a grassy bank along the winding path they undressed. Angela responded to his own eagerness, taking the initiative right from the start. And if there was a heaven like the old man kept harping on about then this was definitely it! She had gone down to him with her soft lips, making loud sucking noises in time with his own grunts of delight, easing up every time she got him close, then going back down to him, playing with him, laughing, providing her own commentary on those occasions when her mouth was empty. He was delirious with pleasure. Even that piercing shriek of shocked female horror took several seconds to penetrate his brain. Then Angela screamed and grabbed her discarded clothing, and he was left to face an irate Miss Titley in his nakedness.

She fled. Later she phoned the Reverend Middlemoor and attempted to explain in her own embarrassed and indignant way on just which part of the male body that precocious whore's lips were fastened. She made herself sufficiently understood and the couple left the vicarage under a cloud. Now they were back, and even if all was not forgiven they would sleep in separate bedrooms because the late summer nights were too chilly to kip under a hedge. And they had important matters to attend to.

The Reverend Middlemoor was in no mood to chair a question time on irrelevant issues. He had done his duty, everybody present had signed a letter and tomorrow they would be posted to London in a secondhand jiffy bag with a gummed economy label advocating recycling paper to save trees. There was no more to be said. He gathered up his papers, glanced once more at his son and hopefully not his future daughter-in-law, and left by the rear exit behind the stage.

'Tomorrow morning,' Glenn Middlemoor breathed to his girlfriend as they mingled with the dispersing, disgruntled crowd.

'Maybe we ought to contact some of the others in this area.' She always felt safer in company on such expeditions; the more the better.

'I already have,' he laughed. 'They're going to make their way individually up to that pheasant pen in Corby Wood. The one where that interfering old bag got savaged by a pack of the keeper's dogs. We meet at noon.'

'Wouldn't it be better after dark?' She wasn't keen to roam the woods at night but a daytime assault seemed to be asking for trouble. That keeper might be around and set his dogs on them.

'Pheasants roost at night, stupid!' He wished at times that Angela wasn't so thick. 'Chuck 'em out into the woods at night and the foxes'll have them. Open the pen up in the daytime and they won't stop flying this side of the river. Got it?'

'They say that there are wolves in the woods.'

'Jeez, you don't believe *that*, do you? That's the sensational press for you! Or it might be a story that Broughton's put around to try to keep people out. If you ask me, the whole business is a hoax deliberately started by that bastard for his own ends. The dogs got Titley, just as they got that Barker boy. They blame the foxes and the mink, and somehow fool the police. But once we've let their pheasants out then there won't be anything to shoot, so Broughton will have to cancel his plans. We'll bankrupt him and he'll have to sell up.'

'Suppose he sets the dogs on *us*?'

'Let the bastard try. We'll have water pistols loaded with ammonia and blind the fuckers!'

She nodded; this whole business sounded just too casual, not enough planning. And lying there on her own in the darkened spare bedroom at the vicarage she heard a distant howling that came from somewhere up by the Corby Wood. It sounded like wolves, but that was impossible. It had to be the dog pack. And that was a very frightening thought also.

Angela kept close to Glenn Middlemoor all the way up to the big wood. They did not enter by the recognized public right of way off the main road but took a short cut across Yates's meadowland, keeping a wary eye out for grazing cattle but there were none in sight.

'Some cows trampled and . . . gored a man to death here,' Angela whispered, shaking.

'More like the bull that they put with them to keep folks away. Just like they used the dogs,' Glenn retorted. 'I noted that my old man didn't include that German bloke in his minute's silence last night. He doesn't like Krauts because he's racist, still fighting the war he never went to. He doesn't like Blacks, either.'

'I think that's disgusting for a man of the church.'

'These vicars are all the same. Believe me, I know 'em better than most. Now, we'd better go carefully from here on. Let's follow this track up to the wood.'

There were three youths and two teenage girls waiting by the entrance to the release pen when Glenn and Angela emerged into the clearing. Scruffy jeans and T-shirts appeared to be the uniform required for this foray. Nodding but not speaking, they glanced furtively, fearfully.

They stood there listening for the rustle of the penned birds skulking in the undergrowth inside the enclosure, but there was only silence. Except for the incessant buzzing of flies. There seemed to be flies everywhere, clouds of bluebottles swarming, settling, feeding.

'Let's take a look.' Glenn stepped forward and produced a pair of strong bolt cutters from the pocket of his jeans. The others watched as he exerted pressure with both hands, straining to cut through the padlock clasp with the small cutters. His features were twisted with the effort and the obsession which drove him on. He grunted and cursed. And then there was a loud snap, followed by 'that's it!'

The gate creaked open and swung on its rusted T-hinges. Everybody stood back, as if to say: Do we *have* to go in there? If we just leave it open the pheasants will find their own way out. Won't they? Looking to the vicar's son for leadership, they subconsciously pandered to him because his father was a man of the cloth, from a kind of inbuilt fear and awe.

'Let's go inside, then.' Glenn Middlemoor stepped into the mesh cage, Angela holding on to his arm, the others following. Pausing, listening again, they swatted at flies that tried to settle on every area of exposed flesh.

'We'll have to start from the other end.' Glenn spoke in a whisper. 'Fan out and keep abreast of one another, then walk back towards the gate like those bloody beaters do. The pheasants are shit-scared, they'll hide rather than fly. And if we don't get 'em out the bloody keeper will just come and shut the pen up again and we'll've wasted our time.'

Reluctantly they shuffled in his wake, following the tall wire fence, treading warily, scratching their legs on wicked trailing briars against which denim was no protection. They were frightened in case the undergrowth might hide poisonous snakes, and clutching ammonia-filled water pistols in sweaty hands for fear of lurking dogs. This might be a decoy by Broughton, a trap set especially for them, trespassers to be savaged by ferocious guard dogs. Glancing behind them, they wondered how much further they had to go before they reached the far end.

Glenn was aware of a smell, one which grew stronger by the second. It was like something decomposing; he reckoned it was probably the stench of the disgusting vermin gibbet at the far end of the wood wafting towards them, that length of rope tied between two trees with rotting crows and grey squirrels hanging from it. On the way back they'd cut it down and –

Angela screamed and clutched at Glenn, almost overbalancing him. Recoiling, bunching, they gasped at the scene which greeted them beyond the wall of blackberry bushes. In the open space devoid of grass where the pheasants fed from the elevated drum feeder, a patch of scratched up soil where the birds dust-bathed in dry weather, pheasants were everywhere – dozens of them, near-featherless poults and more mature cocks, barely recognizable for what they were.

They were dead, every one of them. Lying in heaps, some on their backs, mangled and mauled, headless and half-eaten. The corpses crawled with flies, the meat a greenish colour as it rapidly decomposed in the heatwave and gave off a nauseating stench. It was carnage beyond belief.

'Fucking hell!' One of the youths was backing away, bumping into those behind him. He retched and vomited. 'What the fuck!'

'It's the dogs,' Angela voiced the terror that had haunted her since the previous night when she lay and listened to the bestial howling that came from up here. 'Or the foxes which killed Lucy Titley... as *they* claim!'

'No, that's impossible.' Glenn Middlemoor was staring at the mutilated pheasants as he retreated with the others. 'It's neither dogs nor foxes, I'm sure.'

'What then?' *Come on, sky pilot's son, you tell us since you're so fucking clever.*

'Neither dogs nor foxes could get into an enclosure like this. It's the next best thing to Fort Knox. I tell you what's done this. It's *mink*!'

'Mink! But they're all dead, I read it in the paper...'

'Balls!' Glenn licked his lips and tasted rotting pheasant flesh. 'You kill a few mink but others move in. Remember, we released three hundred from that mink farm only five miles from here that night two years ago.

They breed in the wild, you know. Broughton might claim to have wiped 'em out, but that's just talk. You can take it from me that the mink have found the pheasants up here and it's no trouble for them to scale a mesh fence.'

'Jesus Christ, you really think so?'

'I'm sure of it. Well, at least the birds are out of their misery. I guess we can go now.'

Their relief was combined with regret because they had not struck a personal blow against the Corby owner. And fear too, because they remembered what the mink had done to Brian Barker. *If* it was true; they tried to convince themselves that it was lies, propaganda, until they were clear of the big wood. They kept a wary eye out for Charolais heifers again as they crossed the meadow towards the road, but there was only a carpet of buttercups whose bright yellow flowers were beginning to fade now that summer was in its final stages.

Then back on to the road with its speeding traffic, an everyday world far from the terrors of Corby Wood.

But still the stench of slaughter lingered in their nostrils.

Jim Wilson had left the meeting hall amidst the throng of villagers, an outcast who resented each and every one of them because they despised him and his way of life. Which, he considered, was none of their fucking business. He didn't work – didn't need to, because he did not have a family to support. The council had let him live on in the semi after his mother died, the State paid him for staying on there, and he didn't have to worry about rates. Or heating bills. Just ask and they help you, he'd found out. All of which gave him enough money to continue his own modest lifestyle.

At forty-two he was set in his own ways. He wore the same clothes day after day – body odours were somehow comforting to a loner, like cocking a snoot at society. Balding, he had sharp, angular features and deep-set eyes that flickered furtively. He had once read somewhere that people got to look like the animals they kept. Fine, if he looked like a ferret then he didn't mind. In fact, it was a compliment.

He had done his share of poaching on the Corby estate long before this snob Broughton came to live there. It was much easier in the old days because there were no gamekeepers to look out for, like there were now. Jim never carried a gun. He netted all his rabbits as they bolted from their warrens with a ferret on their tail. Working silently on moonlit nights, he had sometimes accounted for more than he could carry home and had had to make two journeys. Even in those days rabbits were fetching a pound a couple in the market, and sometimes he could earn more in one night than the social security paid him in a week. But all that had come to an end, thanks to the bastard who lived up at the big house now. Rabbiting was too risky on the estate, and on the adjoining lands there had been an outbreak of myxomatosis which had cleared all the conies. So, in effect, his ferrets had become a liability. He didn't even have dead rabbits to feed them on and was forced to buy scraps from the butcher. And what was the point of keeping animals that did not pay?

Jim made up his mind to get rid of his ferrets because the old days would never return. No amount of petitioning by the villagers would turn the estate back to being a sanctuary where a moocher like himself could take all the rabbits he wanted, unhindered. He had taken his four ferrets into market the previous week, hoping to get a tenner for them. There were no buyers because the rabbits were gone. So he brought the hob and three jills home and put them back in the hutch behind the coal bunker. Not only did he have to feed them, they also had to be cleaned out. Well, they'd have to have the chop if nobody wanted them.

It was on his way home from the protest meeting,

dragging his feet, slouching with hunched shoulders and his hands in his pockets, that an idea came to him: a way in which to be rid of his unwanted pets and to get even with that gamekeeper fellow at the same time. He sniggered. That big pen in Corby Wood was full of pheasants, so was the one on Spion Kop and in the smaller wood. Damn it, he'd go up there tonight, and to hell with all this shit about savage animals. The vicar hadn't liked his comment about an exorcism. Well, Jim laughed to himself, he'd do it for the bugger, exorcise the bleedin' pheasants!

The expedition from his council house up to the home covert and its adjoining woods took Jim Wilson the best part of three hours. He was nervous — moonlit nights had become frightening rather than exciting — and he almost changed his mind about the whole business when the foxes started howling. They hadn't used to sound like that, he thought; in winter a dog fox would bark and the vixen would give an unearthly screech in answer, but you never heard them all baying together. They didn't go about in packs, they were loners.

With no small amount of relief he found himself at the big pen. He lowered the sack he was carrying to the ground, groped inside it and drew out a ferret. He threw it over the high fence, then heard it thud into the undergrowth on the other side. Seconds later another followed the first one; two for the big pen, one each for the others. The foxes were howling again and he hurried on his way. Even before he reached the end of the wood he heard the fluttering and screeching of the pheasants inside the release pen as the ferrets began hunting them down; those which jukked on the ground would die tonight, the others when they dropped down from their tree roosts at first light. Oh, sweet Jesus, he was doing more to help the villagers' cause than a thousand petitions and letters to MPs would do!

By three a.m. Jim Wilson was back in his bachelor

bed listening to the howling in the distant woods. And by tomorrow morning there would not be many pheasants left alive on the estate!

'Well, we'll have to sell up then, won't we?' Pamela Broughton failed to keep a note of relief out of her voice. She had stayed on at Corby through this summer of traumas for no logical reason, and now they would have no alternative but to go. She felt like a soldier who had contemplated desertion at the battlefront only to hear his commanding officer give the order to retreat.

'Christ, it's crazy!' John Broughton wilted momentarily, his determination flagging at this latest setback, but suddenly he was stubborn and fighting again. 'One thing after another. Vogt has chickened out after Rubisch's death, so we don't have any wealthy overseas sportsmen flocking here. But it doesn't matter anyway because all our pheasants are dead, killed by marauding *ferrets*! We don't have any sport to sell, unless we buy in about three thousand surplus adult birds from any game farmer with stock left to sell at about two quid a bird. That's another six grand on top of our losses. The bank won't sanction it. And there's no guarantee that if we could find the pheasants we need, something wouldn't happen to *them*! But we're not beaten. No, by Christ, we're not done for yet!'

'Oh?' She felt her hopes plummeting. 'What's left in your bag of tricks then, John?'

'We'll open up Corby House to the public,' he said.

'Sir Thomas Corby tried that. It was an unmitigated disaster. It isn't a stately home, just a country mansion, and there are hundreds up and down the country struggling to survive on a dwindling tourist trade.'

'But we're in the bloody news!' he shouted. 'We've hit the headlines – the Corby Curse and all that stuff. The crowds will flock here just as if we were Borley Rectory risen up out of its ashes!'

'And then we'll probably have a fire, too', she

snapped. 'Be reasonable, John. Unless we can get our money back we'll go bankrupt. We might just find a buyer if we put it on the market now.'

'No.' He was suddenly exultant. 'We can get the tourists here on an end-of-season fling, I'm sure. And there are still enough wild pheasants in the woods to sell a few days' shooting on a limited basis. If we can struggle through to next year, then we'll rebuild the sporting side. Blast those ferrets! I'm sure they were put in the release pens deliberately. I can't blame Shank, he's overworked as it is; he can't sit up in the woods all night watching his birds. But if you want to go back to London, don't let me stop you.'

'I might just do that.' Her words lacked conviction.

'We're on the ropes.' He was staring out of the window, visualising the wide driveway immediately below the house packed with visitors' cars. 'But we're not down and out yet!'

She wasn't listening. The Corby Curse was alive; only death could result from attempting to defy it.

14

Brenda Warner was looking forward to next week when school started again. As a single parent with a six-year-old boy, school holidays could be very tiresome. Particularly the summer ones — they seemed to go on for months. At least in term time she had a few hours to herself each day.

At twenty-six, Brenda had a decidedly worn look about her. Her attractive features were spoiled by lines which seemed to etch deeper each year, her once shapely figure had been ruined by a diet of chips and cheap junk food, and she had to struggle into second-hand clothes from the Oxfam shop. She had no money, apart from her weekly allowance from the State, and no freedom. A victim of circumstances, her misfortunes had left their mark on her and she had resigned herself to a bare existence in a council flat in Warwick.

Barry could be very trying most of the time, she thought. Nowadays it wasn't safe to turn him out to play with the other kids in the park behind the flat; she had to go with him, push the rusted swing for him, stand for interminable periods by the creaking roundabout, help to give it momentum if there weren't other children around. Last week she had been down to the park every day for several hours; if she didn't have a change of scenery she would go mad. Holidays were out of the question, but she felt duty bound to give her son an outing of some kind. Which was why she had scraped enough for the bus fare out to Corby village and fifty pence admittance to the big house. Children were free, which was an added bonus, and by bringing sandwiches and a flask she hoped to complete the excursion for under a fiver. She could just about afford an ice cream for Barry if she went without herself. Except that they didn't sell ices here. In fact, the place was a bloody con, just a rather large house with grounds that were in need of attention.

She spent the first hour down by the lake. There were some ducks and Barry wanted to feed them.

'We don't have anything to feed them with, dear,' she explained for the third time. 'We can't afford to give them our sandwiches else we'll go hungry.'

'I don't mind, Mum. I'm not hungry anyway.' He was going to get petulant in a minute, she could tell. That would mean a slap and a crying session, and they might as well have stopped at home.

'All right, just one then. And you mind you don't fall in.'

He snatched the furling cheese sandwich out of her

hand and went back to the water's edge. Five mallard quacked loudly in anticipation of food and began to swim towards the shore.

Brenda reflected with bitterness upon her lot in life. It was like a cancer inside her eating her away. She blamed herself mostly. She had given up hating Mark years ago. It was all her own fault. One evening out with a man she had never met before, an hour's uncontrolled passion, and years in which to repent in bored and poverty-stricken leisure.

Mark was handsome, any girl would have fallen for him. Tall and dark-haired, well-spoken. He had chatted her up at the supermarket where she worked on the checkout and asked her if she was free that evening. She was, and she had gone out with him. He was too good to be true: he was educated, sales manager for some big firm. So he had said. His name might not even have been Mark. It probably wasn't. She couldn't understand why a bloke like that was wasting his time with a shopgirl but she wasn't complaining. She knew now, all right; stopping off overnight on his travels, and a bit on the side to pass the time.

Barry was breaking the bread into small pieces and throwing them to the ducks. Now the birds were waddling ashore. They were making an awful lot of noise and sounded angry. Ungrateful buggers, she thought.

It was the old story, nothing new, and she had fallen for it all along. A meal at a restaurant in town, more than she was accustomed to drinking. In fact, she usually only drank shandies. Laughing at his repertoire of jokes. A quick drink in a pub – he had persuaded her to have a whisky – and then a ride out into the countryside. They had parked up in a quiet lane. Even so, she had made up her mind that it wasn't going to be anything more than a snogging session. All right, a feel then. Her nipples had always been her weakness; when she was sixteen Brenda had surrendered her virginity because a boy had stroked them. It was no different now. Mark's soft slender fingers caressed them, had them firmly erect within seconds. She made a token protest when his hand slid between her thighs but then she was groaning her pleasure. She even helped him to remove her clothing and spread herself in readiness for him. One minor point, she told him, she wasn't on the Pill so perhaps he should wear something. He hadn't got any condoms with him, never *dreamed* that he might have need of them. But not to worry, he would withdraw in plenty of time. He was so reassuring and she wanted it as badly as he did. Half an hour of fiery passion; she orgasmed twice and might have made it a third time, holding him close, her fingernails digging deep into his bare back as he bucked and thrust, then finally lay spent on top of her. He had not withdrawn but maybe it would be all right. It wasn't, but by then Mark wasn't around and she had never heard from him since. Which was why she was here at Corby House today, giving the result of that night of passion a sandwich with which to feed the ducks.

Suddenly Barry screamed and came running towards her, crying and holding up a finger. Mallard quacked after him; one pecked his bare legs and made him shriek again.

'Get away. Shoo!' Brenda was on her feet, kicking the ducks away. They fluttered and kept their distance but did not retreat to the safety of the water. Bunched, they were watching with evil black glittering eyes.

'Come on, luv. Let mummy see.' Holding him to her, she examined the injured finger. It was red. It might bruise later but the skin wasn't broken. 'There, you'll be all right.'

'I don't like ducks.' He had stopped crying and was sullen now. Which boded ill for the rest of the day. 'I want to go home.'

'The bus doesn't go until five o'clock.' She led him away, glancing back to make sure that those ducks were not about to attack again. They were still there, watching, a kind of sadistic satisfaction in their expressions. 'Come on, we'll go into the house and see what's to see there.'

'I don't want to go into the house.'

'Well, we can always come back outside if we don't like it.' Damn those ducks, she thought. We could have done without this.

Brenda was suddenly aware that she and her son were the only visitors. A couple of parked cars stood outside but they probably belonged to the owners. The empty hallway made her feel an intruder. There was a table with some duplicated pamphlets on it. She picked one up and was grateful when Barry said, 'There's nobody around,' and his complaining voice brought footsteps hurrying down the stairs.

'Good morning.' Pamela Broughton smiled and hurried to the table. 'Ah, I see you've taken a leaflet. Good. Carry on, up the stairs and then down the rear ones, which will bring you to the west wing.'

'Isn't there a guide?' This was all very amateurish, and a quick glance showed Brenda that there wasn't much in the leaflet, just a plan of the house, a visitor's route and a couple of paragraphs relating the history of the place. The rear page was devoted to the grounds. There was no mention of the curse or whatever it was that had been on telly the other night.

'I'm afraid there isn't a guide.' She was haughty because a guide would have been superfluous. 'Visitors are allowed to go round on their own. Which they aren't at most country houses.' *Take it or leave it*.

It wasn't worth arguing about. Brenda held Barry's hand firmly and steered him towards the stairs. He was dragging his feet, determined to be awkward. 'Let's see what we can find upstairs.' Which wouldn't be a lot judging by what they had seen downstairs, she reckoned. That woman was standing watching them as if she resented their intrusion on her privacy.

At the top of the stairs was a wide uncarpeted landing

with rooms leading off, the doors open in readiness. Some nice antique furniture, she noted, and a bedroom with a four-poster and a cracked water jug on the table beside it. If it had not been for the dense rhododendrons nearly as high as the window she might have had a panoramic view of the grounds.

'Mummy, let's go outside.'

'In a minute. If we follow this route, see those arrows, then it brings us back outside. Now, just be quiet else the woman downstairs will be cross.'

'I think she's cross already.'

'Sshh!' Children were renowned for speaking the truth but sometimes it could be embarrassing. 'Oh, look up there, Barry, at those lovely pistols on the wall.'

In fact the pistols on display were shabby. They might have come from a junk shop and had not been restored. The focal point of this small high-ceilinged room, a typewritten card on the table to the effect that this was the late Sir Thomas Corby's bedroom. Somebody had removed the bed. It was bare and uninteresting.

'Mummy, let's go.'

'We're nearly finished.' Ten minutes from the start, Brenda was already in sight of the rear stairway. It did not match the rest of the woodwork and had probably been put in fairly recently in order to satisfy fire regulations. She wondered how they were going to pass the rest of the day; certainly they weren't going back to the lake and those bad-tempered ducks.

'What's that, Mummy?'

'What, luv?'

'That noise.' Brenda heard it now, a kind of light drumming that seemed to come from up above. A fast scurrying that gathered force. Louder. And louder.

'What is it, Mummy?' Barry was clinging to her, pulling at her. She resisted the urge to give him a slap. He annoyed her when he got in one of these cloying moods. 'Mummy, it isn't thunder, is it?'

At first she thought it might have been a roll of distant

thunder but the sound, the volume, was wrong. And whatever it was it was indoors, in the room directly above, which was probably an attic.

'Sshh! Be quiet a minute, let me listen.'

She looked up. The ceiling above seemed to vibrate and an oak beam was trembling. There was a scurrying noise, like hundreds, thousands, of tiny feet going round and round. *Trapped and looking for a way out!*

'I think we'd better go outside.' Her skin was prickling. There was a mounting inexplicable fear taking a grip on her that was likely to escalate into panic at any second. That business with the ducks had unnerved both of them; there were wild stories on the television and in the papers about animals attacking humans here, foxes behaving like wolves, mink killing a boy. 'Come on, let's go.'

And then Barry was screaming for the second time that day. A loft trapdoor in the far corner of the ceiling had suddenly dropped, swinging on its hinges. And through the gap tumbled a living shower of greyish-brown creatures that squeaked as they piled and bounced on the floor; then rolled and scurried. Rats!

Brenda lifted up her son, snatched him clear of the living, moving carpet of rodents and held him aloft. Now she was screaming, piercing shrieks, first of fear, then of pain as sharp teeth bit her ankles. The rats were milling all around, squeaking, biting. Attacking. She kicked out in her panic and sent some flying, but they were replaced immediately by others. *And they were still showering through that square hole up above where their sheer weight of numbers had ripped the bolt from its fittings.*

She felt their sharp claws on her legs, shredding her tights as they secured a hold. They began climbing up. *Oh, God, no! Please spare my child!*

Oblivious to the pain now, her only thought was to reach that flight of stairs, somehow to carry Barry to safety. But the rats were swarming up beneath her

Oxfam cord skirt, tearing at her knickers, pulling out her pubic hair in tufts as they fought to feed on the tenderest part of her anatomy. She felt the warmth of her own blood trickling down her legs as she tried to stagger to safety. Barry was yelling, wriggling in his fear; he might overbalance her at any second. They were treading on bodies that crunched and squelched, and were screaming too.

And then she lost her balance, unable to prevent herself from falling. The screeching child slipped from her hold. Her own landing was soft, but then the rats were swarming all over her. She had been bitten everywhere. Blood was pouring down over her eyes, obscuring her vision. She tried to kick and punch but the weight of her attackers pinioned her arms and legs. One brief view of Barry showed her a bloody mulch beneath the squirming creatures that buried him, eating him as he lived. And then he was gone.

Whimpering, not fighting them any more because she had resigned herself to her terrible fate, she blamed herself because she had let Mark do what he wanted that night and it had led to this awful ending – a child born to die horribly with her. It was her own fault. The rats were punishing her for what she had done, eating the flesh from her bones. She prayed for death. They were at her throat now, biting deep, gnawing and pulling until the blood started to spurt, bathing them crimson.

Brenda never heard the heavy footsteps charging up the stairs, or Pamela Broughton's scream. Gordon Shank wielded a heavy stick as he waded into the rodent army which had lain hidden and multiplying up in the attics for years.

Suddenly the rats were gone. As one they turned and scurried for the stairway, a verminous river in full spate pouring down the steps, spilling into the corridor below, streaming out into the bright sunshine, fleeing in every direction. Their hour of freedom was nigh; too long had they skulked indoors in fear of man. Now they were unleashed upon the open countryside, a strange environment where they must hide again. But they had allies, for the Corby Curse had called them over the centuries, a summons which they dared not disobey.

Rats rustled the trailing boughs of the rhododendrons and darted across the open lawns. Some headed for the woods, others towards the lake and the river. Startled mallard at the water's edge took wing in fright and flew to safety. Small birds twittered their fear in the topmost branches of trees. And then the countryside swallowed and hid the creatures, protecting them. For the animal army had swelled its ranks in the war to vanquish man from the Corby lands.

15

'I can't stand it any longer!' If it had not been for the fact that Gordon, Jill and Gary Shank were in the kitchen of Corby House, Pamela would have given way to hysteria. White-faced, looking angrily at John, she averted her gaze from the others. 'I, for one, am leaving. Tomorrow!'

Jill Shank glanced at Gordon and decided to remain silent. It was akin to a recording of the conversation which had taken place in the gamekeeper's cottage an hour ago, a surrender by the womenfolk. Only the men were determined to stay and fight.

They would never forget yesterday, the place suddenly alive with rats, scurrying, squeaking, evil, verminous creatures leaving the buildings *en masse* as though the legendary piper was calling them. Then disappearing; that was the most worrying factor. They sensed that *they* had not given up, just gone into hiding, waiting for the call to mass and kill again.

Oh, God, it was awful! First the ambulance and police, then the television news crew, who were only interested in the gory details. Reporters pestering, hanging about. If they couldn't obtain an interview they wrote one all the same. Both Jill and Pamela knew that they had reached the limit of their personal endurance. The killings weren't going to stop now; the Curse was alive, it would not rest until it had killed them all. Jill's only consolation was that Claire was still staying with her parents. And she wouldn't be coming back here. No way. If she missed school when it started next week, too bloody bad! She would phone the education authority to try to get her daughter transferred to a school close to where she was staying. In the meantime this was the crunch meeting, the womenfolk telling their men that they were leaving Corby. Jill's only problem was Gary. She was not going to sacrifice her son to whatever was going on here. Which was why she would probably stay in the end, under protest.

'Let's look at the situation *logically*.' John Broughton was desperate, clinging to his tottering empire that was crumbling all about him.

'Logically!' Pamela snapped angrily. 'There's no *logic* here, John. We are up against an evil force which is invincible. The animals have gone crazy and – I –'

'We'll kill 'em, wipe out the lot.' He was beginning to shout. 'We'll destroy every last one of 'em, if I have to do it myself.'

'Which is impossible!' she retorted.

'We killed the mink. The crows are dead in their hundreds. The council pest officer will eradicate the rats. We'll call in the Fox Club to drive the woods and shoot every fox that shows itself.'

'I've been in touch with the fox boys.' Shank was referring to the group of locals who organised fox drives during the winter months for the benefit of farmers in the district. 'They won't entertain the idea, because the undergrowth is too thick for the beaters at this time of year. Not just that, they're shit-scared, and who wouldn't be after what happened to the mink hounds? There's nothing doing there, the Fox Club won't help.' He licked his lips nervously. He was siding with Pamela and Jill, and the boss would hate him for that, maybe sack him. But unemployment was preferable to death.

'Sod 'em then.' Broughton lit a cigarette, took the smoke deep down into his lungs, then expelled it slowly. 'Shooting foxes is fine but we can't guarantee to get the lot that way, there's always the odd cunning one that will slip back and avoid the guns, or be missed. I'm talking about a method which is guaranteed to exterminate the bastards. Bait 'em with strychnine!'

'Strychnine!' Gordon Shank paled. He began to tremble visibly. 'You can't do that. Strychnine never dies, and you don't know where it's going to end up.'

'And I don't bloody well care!' Broughton leaned forward, hands spread on the scrubbed table top, the veins in his neck corded. 'As I said, we'll wipe out everything. And start again.'

There was silence. Everybody in the room looked at one another. A death sentence had been pronounced and it might not stop at animals. Strychnine could be carried in various ways and a couple of grains were fatal to a human being. Broughton struggled to get himself under control, sensing a revolt. He might push these others too far, he realised. His servants, his gardeners had left. He could not survive without Shank and it was a certain fact that no other gamekeeper would take the job on. Pamela would leave this time – he did not mind that. But not Gordon. Please!

'There's nothing left to fight for,' Pamela said, her voice so low that it was scarcely audible. 'Your shooting enterprise is finished and it's a certainty that we'll never get another tourist within half a mile of the house after yesterday!' Oh, Christ, she would never get that upstairs scene out of her mind, it would be a waking and sleeping nightmare for the rest of her life. That room, those corpses eaten down to their bones, blood everywhere. 'Give in whilst you're still alive, John.'

'No,' he hissed, turning his gaze back to the keeper. 'I'm not going to be beaten by a load of animals. What about *you*, Shank?' The 'Gordon' was dropped, the boss was ready to fire his employee if necessary. 'Well?'

'All right.' He wanted to say 'fuck off' but it wouldn't come. In self-humiliation he sensed Jill's anger, Pamela's contempt. But in this instance he would be a coward whether he stayed or left. 'I'll give it one last go, but what the hell for I don't know because there will be nothing left in the end.'

'Damn it!' Broughton was suddenly near-euphoric now that he had an ally. 'We'll rebuild. From scratch. There are enough wild pheasants left here to sell some shoot days on a small scale, maybe enough to keep the ship afloat. Get over this hurdle and we'll be okay, you see if I'm not right.'

'You're mad.' Pamela spoke calmly, not in anger, just making a statement. She gave a sigh, and then, 'Well, I'm going to start packing. It seems that everybody is free to stay or leave. I'm leaving within the hour.'

Jill Shank swallowed. A dilemma; Claire was safe, and if Gary had been somewhere else she would have left too. Gordon could please himself. But he had made the decision to remain and she knew that there was no way she would drag her son away. So she would stay here in this place of death where wild carnivores ruled.

Pamela brushed past them, closing the door behind her. Talk about me if you like, she thought, I don't want to hear. Up the stairs; one last time. She wasn't coming back. Ever.

The bedroom was full of insects. Corn flies swarmed all over the walls like unsightly patches of rising damp and some wasps buzzed angrily on the window panes. She watched them carefully as she began tossing clothes into an open suitcase on the bed and wondered where that filthy spider had got to. They all seemed oblivious to her, as if they thought, you're leaving, you're spared. As if they were already taking over the house.

She was hurrying now. Just take the essentials, she told herself. The rest can be sent on afterwards. She forced herself to think of London, a concrete world divorced from this seething terror, where the only birds were pigeons in Trafalgar Square and starlings fouling the buildings in winter. A few cats and dogs, all the other animals were caged in the zoo, where they could not harm anybody.

Back down the stairs, carrying a suitcase, she glanced towards the closed kitchen door. No voices came from within and she did not know whether the others were still there; she did not care. No farewells, just a hurried exit. *Goodbye Corby, it has* not *been nice knowing you.*

Outside she paused on the steps and saw the Justy shimmering in the sunlight as though beckoning her. Five minutes and she would be away from this place of evil for good. The Curse had won. She didn't care. The driver's door hung open, the seat belt had fallen and stopped it from closing when she had got out earlier. In London you locked and checked all your car doors before you left it; she would have to pick up the habit again. And then she noticed something moving on the lawn.

At first she thought it was an optical illusion, a patch of sun-browned grass appearing to unfurl, perhaps a mole burrowing up from beneath. Long and slender, uncoiling, it stretched out until she could see the flat head, the dark 'V' markings on its body. Oh, no *an adder, like the one that had attacked Miss Titley that day back in the spring*!

She almost turned and ran back into the house. Only the thought of what lay indoors prevented her. Not just those insects, nor the dreadful memory of the rats, more the impending threat; the thought of what still lurked there unseen. Half-turning, she paused, and stood watching the snake in fascinated horror.

It was fully twenty yards away, close to the rhododendrons. In all probability it had just crawled out from beneath the shady foliage to bask in the sunshine. Motionless now, fully extended – it had not even seen her. It looked drowsy. Sun-basking, as she had thought.

She found herself walking forward stealthily on the balls of her feet, the weight of the suitcase forgotten. hurrying, trying not to panic, she headed towards the open car door. *Quickly*! Her heart was tip-tapping fast and she was aware of the claminess of her body. Her eyes never once left that reptile. Still it did not move. She made it to the car, fumbled her luggage over into the rear, and felt it slide off the seat and wedge itself. It didn't matter. She got in, slammed the door. It bounced open off the seat belt; she cursed, pulled the webbing clear and shut the door firmly. This time it held, thank God.

Memories of that night made her brace herself for swarms of flying objects of various sizes throwing themselves frenziedly at the windscreen. There were none, not even an angry wasp. Firing the engine, revving it, she looked across at the adder again. It was still there, had not even raised its head at the sound of the car starting up. Because she was leaving. *They were letting her go*.

No, it would not be as easy as that, she thought. They were playing with her, a sadistic game. Any second a stag would come hurtling out of the bushes and throw itself at the radiator grill. The badger, too. Again she glanced at the snake and thought about running over it, one last gesture of revenge as she took a wide sweep over the hard-baked lawn. *No, don't even think it, that's asking for trouble. Go whilst you still can*.

A final glance in her rear mirror: the creature was still there, perhaps it had squirmed out of its lair to die in the sunshine. If it had, then that was fine. She didn't care now. On down the driveway, a cloud of dust swirling in her wake. She winced on every bend but there was no sign of life, then sighed audibly as she emerged on to open ground. Yates's meadow was on her left now, behind the hedge where Rubisch had died, the field where those crows had mobbed the keeper's boy. She was sweating but afraid to open the window.

Past the Shanks' cottage. She did not even look towards it because she knew that they were still up at the house being persuaded to remain on one final mission of revenge. The donkey was looking over the stile. It drew back its lips and seemed to leer evilly at her. She reached the spot where Peach had died. Driving fast, recklessly, she slowed only when she came to the cattle grid, rattling it noisily in a final farewell to everything that she was leaving behind.

Almost crying her relief aloud, waiting for a gap in the speeding traffic, she eased her way out on to the busy road, catching up the Metro ahead of her. *I've done it! Thank goodness, I've escaped!*

It was hot, and now she could wind the window down. By the time she was on the M1 the sky was heavy and overcast, the sunshine hazy. The weather was changing, she could feel it. The heat had hit a peak, a last fling of summer that had spilled over into autumn, but soon it would rain. Today possibly. She did not care; in London you did not notice the weather like you did in the countryside.

They would all die back at Corby, every one of those who had elected or been talked into remaining. She felt sorry for Jill and the boy, it wasn't their fault, they were victims of circumstances. Gordon did not matter to her and neither did John now. Her husband was to blame, he had brought all this about. A selfish, obsessional pig, he just wanted to kill animals and birds and now they were going to kill him.

She reflected, for the benefit of her conscience, that

she would have left him anyway, sooner or later, because there was nothing left for either of them in their empty relationship. They had gone their own separate ways a long time ago. If he died now then it was his own fault. Like suicide.

Rainspots hit the windscreen, startling her momentarily, yet another reminder of those fluttering insects that night. She laughed her contempt for herself and switched on the wipers. The sky ahead was a purple bordering on black. A jagged arrow of fire split it open. One hell of a storm up ahead; everything was changing. Gone was the summer and with it everything she wanted to forget.

Lines of shimmering headlights scintillated the downpour. The rush of water and spray gave her the feeling that she was in a speedboat, another reminder of the past: that crazy trip across the bay when they were on their honeymoon, and she screamed to John to slow up before they capsized. He did not, but they arrived safely back in the harbour. Broughton's luck, he called it. But that luck was running out now.

She wanted to move back into the centre lane but there wasn't a gap. Nobody was slowing, everybody aquaplaning, throwing up blinding spray. The wipers were on full speed but even that was not enough. She reckoned the coach in front was doing a ton, as she was, throwing back oil and filth that had lain on the tarmac surface for weeks.

She was trying to drop back, just in case. The car immediately behind her was too close but there was nothing she could do about it. Listening to the swishing of tyres, the rain on the roof, the . . .

A sound that somehow wasn't quite right. Her ears picked it up, queried it. Like something slithering on the back seat. That bloody suitcase was sliding out of its wedge, she decided, and would thump on to the floor at any second. She reached behind her with her left hand and tried to move it back. But it wasn't the case because it was still stuck firmly.

And that was when the snakes bit her.

Turning, screaming, she saw them before the Justy went out of control – a writhing mass of entwined serpents, a nest of adders which had lain camouflaged on the brown seat cover, sleeping in the heat and then being aroused by the drop in temperature.

Aroused and angry, they struck as one at the tender human flesh which poked threateningly at them.

Pamela Broughton was still screaming her terror when the car clipped the rear of the coach in front and slewed across the central reservation

16

John Broughton was numbed by the news of Pamela's death. A police car arrived at Corby House just after darkness fell and the young constable broke the news. The Justy had been crushed beneath an oncoming tanker and it had taken the fire crew two hours to cut the mangled body out.

He was shocked because you never believed that such things happen to you or your kin. And saddened, but the grief was tempered by the knowledge that their marriage was over, had been for some time. Two people living together, pretending for no other reason than that it was convenient to go on in that way. Now it was all over. Pamela would not be coming back.

He would tell the Shanks tomorrow; it was none of their business and he did not seek sympathy. In the meantime he was alone. Really alone.

He poured himself a double brandy, knowing that he

had to pull himself together. Things were bad, there was no point in trying to deny that. The chips were down, he had his back to the wall. But he was more determined than ever to fight.

Another brandy and he felt better. At least it was *finis*, no long-drawn-out divorce procedures, no explaining to do. Callous, but it was nice and easy. And, by God, he was going to fulfil his ambition as far as the Corby estate was concerned, it was going to be the premier shooting estate in the country. Like Holkham. Or Sandringham. The place where nobility came for their sport, where wealthy foreigners paid fifteen pounds for the privilege of shooting every pheasant, a day that cost well into four figures and they were satisfied that their money was well spent. Prestigious. His own name would go down in sporting history, his picture in the annals of shooting.

But first they had to wipe out virtually every living creature in the area. Shank would spend tomorrow putting out poisoned bait. That would account for the foxes and any corvines that remained after the assault with alpha chloralose. The pest control officer ought to be able to eliminate the rats; damn it, the fellow had spent two days baiting them. The deer would be culled ruthlessly, another job for Shank. A week maybe and there ought not to be much left living in these woods and fields. Just the wild pheasants, and they would be dealt with in a month's time when the shooting season began. Then the cycle would begin again, with fresh blood introduced. No real problem.

He lay on the bed but he did not sleep because his mind was too active. Lying there in the darkened room, he listened to the fox packs howling, disturbing the peace and quiet of the nocturnal countryside. Moths fluttered against the window but they couldn't get in. Tomorrow night there would not be many foxes left to howl, the strychnine would surely have done its work. He was looking forward to lying here and hearing nothing but the silence and knowing that the battle was almost won.

It was one of those troublesome, untidy days. The telephone rang every few minutes so that in the end he left the receiver off. Messages of sympathy which he didn't want. *Tell me at the funeral because I'm putting a day aside to listen.*

Gordon Shank was shocked but he'd convinced him that life had to go on. Damn it, anybody would think that the gamekeeper fancied Pamela! Good luck to him if he had, but he had left it a bit late. That fox bait had to be put out today, whatever.

Towards the middle of the morning the council pest officer rang the front doorbell. A small man with greying hair and an expression that might have belonged to an undertaker, he somehow looked comical in his bright orange overalls.

'Excuse me, sir,' he mumbled, so that Broughton wanted to shout at him to speak up. 'I've checked all the baiting points that I put down the last two days. *Not a single one has been touched!*'

John Broughton felt the hairs on the nape of his neck prickle. It was impossible, there were hundreds of rats around, they had eaten a woman and her child.

'Perhaps they've all left. Rats will sometimes vacate premises for no apparent reason and move on somewhere else. There are innumerable reports of sightings of armies of rats on the move.'

'No, sir, they haven't gone. There are plenty of fresh droppings!'

'Then where are the devils?' He raised his voice in anger and frustration. And fear.

'Search me, sir.'

'You'd better find 'em, then.'

'I can't do more than put bait down.' It was veiled defiance: *Don't you bloody well try to tell me my job, even if you are the bleedin' lord of the manor.* 'I'll 'ave to come and check 'em again tomorrow. Rats are cunning, maybe they're suspicious and it'll take a day or two for 'em to get used to the baiting points.'

'All right, check again tomorrow. But surely you've *seen* the odd rat?'

'No, sir. Nor 'eard 'em. Wherever the buggers are, they're layin' up real close.'

Broughton felt uneasy. The rats should be taking *some* of the bait. It was uncanny. But he had no alternative, he had to leave it to the man from the council and hope for better news tomorrow.

During the late afternoon he drove down to the gamekeeper's cottage. The Land Rover was parked outside. Dogs barked from their kennels but none were running loose. Gordon Shank wasn't taking any chances of them finding some of the strychnine bait.

The keeper appeared in the doorway, shirtsleeved, dishevelled, grimed and sweating. Leaning against the lintel, he was weary and demoralized, hating what he had done today. He nodded, anticipating the question, but did not speak.

'Well done.' For a fleeting moment Broughton experienced guilt. He had ordered his servant to commit a despicable act. But he was being paid to do it, even if it was against the law.

'Forty baits.' Shank's tone was abrupt, almost rebellious. 'Christ, I'm dreading tomorrow! Half of 'em we'll never find, they'll crawl away to die. Crows, too. Something will feed off the corpses, then off *them*, too, when they die. There's no end to it.'

John Broughton nodded. 'It's the only way,' he said, and it sounded weak, an excuse. He was trying to see past Gordon into the cottage but the interior was dark; he sensed an empty living room. Jill was probably upstairs, he thought, maybe grieving more than he was over Pamela's death. An awkward silence ensued. Both men stared down at the ground.

'And if this doesn't do the trick?' The keeper looked up. There was an edge to his voice.

'It will,' Broughton said, turning away. 'I'll see you tomorrow morning, Gordon, after you've been the rounds.'

The sunshine was gone. Now there were broken clouds where for weeks there had been endless blue skies. It had rained in the night but that bad thunderstorm had missed Corby. The depressing greyness everywhere got to him. He drove back to the house. Tomorrow would be the crunch. And he could not get those rats off his mind, how they had scorned the tempting bait. But there was still time even if it was running out.

Night again. John Broughton took the phone off the hook and went upstairs. The bedroom windowsill was layered with dead insects: corn flies, bluebottles, a few wasps. The drop in temperature had been enough to kill them, or perhaps they had completed their lifespan. Tiny bodies all over the floor crunched under his feet when he moved. He found it encouraging because any creature, however insignificant, that died on Corby lands was a bonus. Maybe the rats were dying, too. And the foxes, tonight for sure.

A sudden thought made him go back downstairs into the gunroom, unlock a mahogany cabinet and take down an exquisite double-barrelled shotgun with intricate engraving on the action and a beautifully grained and polished stock. A Purdey, one of a pair; the other was in the rack. Fifteen grand the pair. Its very feel, its perfect balance, was comforting. He took a box of cartridges off the shelf and relocked the cupboard.

Back in the bedroom he propped the gun in a corner, the shells on the floor next to it. Just in case. Guns were part of him, an extension of his own body; he felt incomplete without one. Then he lay back on the bed and switched off the light.

A silvery darkness, an eerie light, came through the

closed curtains, because it was full moon again. Another cycle was complete.

Listening, he braced himself for the vulpine chorus. But it wouldn't happen, would it? Because they were too busy gorging themselves on the poisoned meat. And then they would die an agonising death. He wondered how long it took a fox to die from strychnine poisoning. Not long, surely. It depended how much of the stuff Shank had used; he had told him to use plenty.

Something knocked the window and made him jump. A bat. He waited for it to fly at the glass again but it didn't. Probably it had realised the futility of another attempt and flitted off somewhere. His thoughts were erratic. It was like talking for the sake of it because you were nervous. Tomorrow he would sweep up all those dead insects and burn them. Pamela would have gone hysterical over them but she wasn't here any more. He wondered about her accident, how the Justy had come to career across the central reservation. She was a good driver, so it was obviously some mechanical fault. The police would doubtless check the vehicle over and discover it. It might have been caused by that stag. If so, the animals had got their revenge on her. But right now he was evening the score; he pictured a pack of foxes quarrelling and fighting over a pile of sheep's intestines, slurping it down. Then rolling over, writhing, dying. Oh, Jesus, how he'd love to watch the bastards die!

And then the howling started up. At first it was a lone mournful cry like that of a bored chained-up dog. There was an old saying that when a dog howled somebody was going to die. John Broughton tensed and felt for the light-pull, then snatched his hand away. Putting on the light wasn't going to help anybody, he decided. A resonant fox cry rose to a pitch, died down, then began again. Just one beast . . . the last one left alive, the corpses of its fellow scavengers stretched out around it. A lament of death.

It was but momentary euphoria for Broughton.

Within seconds the howling was taken up – louder, in an angry chorus that shook the still night air. The hunting cry, filled with lust and hatred, sounded as if the long dead wolves of the Corby forests had returned to savage man, who had exterminated them. It was nearer now, as if the beasts were converging on the house, surrounding it, baying at him. *You're trapped, John Broughton. We will wait until you emerge. Or else you can stay indoors and die of starvation.*

Don't be bloody stupid, he told himself. There was a telephone downstairs – he could have help here within minutes. He cursed himself for not having had an extension fitted by the bedside. He had meant to, but had never got round to it because there had been so many macabre distractions. Not that it mattered, because it was quite safe to go downstairs. The bloody foxes couldn't get in the house. *But something else might be inside waiting for him.*

Then he remembered the gun. With a surge of hope and excitement, he threw off the bedclothes and padded across the room to where the barrels shone in the wan moonlight. He picked up the weapon and felt a renewed confidence at the coldness of the steel, the way the Purdey became part of him instantly. A sort of electrification of his whole system dispelled fear. Man was again the hunter, those foxes outside his prey.

He savoured the loading, dropping two cartridges into the breech, hearing the soft click of well-oiled metal as he closed it. He resisted the temptation to push the safety catch forward; you always kept your gun on safe until you were ready to fire.

Gently he parted the curtains and peered out. The landscape was black and silver. The shadows from the rhododendrons fell across the lawn, forming weird shapes. There was a sudden silence, as though the beasts of the night were drawing breath for another vocal onslaught. Their last – it had to be, for they knew they could not survive the strychnine much longer.

Waiting, easing the sash up, pushing the window open, hearing it creak, he was aware of the cool air on his face. An empty world, there was nothing out there, it was all in his imagination.

The shadows moved, a blackness that emerged into the open and turned silver. Pointed ears erect, jaws wide: they were crouching as if they were going to spring up at the open window. He caught his breath as he counted them. *Six*. There might have been another skulking in the deep shadows behind but he could not be sure. Lean and hungry shapes that were still to feast.

Perfectly coordinated their howl that might have been rehearsed a thousand times to attain that degree of precision – a living, evil force directed at the human watcher. He smelled their fetid, rancid odour and recoiled. For a moment he almost panicked, and then he was bringing the gun up to his shoulder, aligning it on the nearest fox.

His finger rested on the trigger but did not take the pressure. Aiming but not firing, he was afraid in case they were impervious to leaden death. Ballistics registered in his confused mind. The cartridges in the gun were number sixes – small-bird shot that was only suitable for partridge or pheasant. The range was thirty yards – sixes would not kill at that distance even if the pellets penetrated a vital organ. Buckshot, SSG, would have dropped a wild boar at that range. But he had no large-shot size, only sixes. A wounding at the very most. Which meant a crazed injured animal that would fight until it died. So John Broughton hesitated.

They had seen him, there was no doubt about that. Pinpoints of eyes glinted redly, burning into him. Yellowed fangs dripped stinking saliva. Starving beasts, they saw their prey and made ready for the kill. But they could not reach him, he knew, any more than his light-shot charge could slay them. Necks stretched, they were starting to howl their anger and frustration yet again.

He fired on impulse, squeezing the trigger before he realized it. The shattering report took him by surprise, pushing him back a foot or so, and the gun barrels jumped upwards. He did not know whether he had hit or missed until he heard an awful scream that surely came from no living creature, a cry that embodied the ultimate in rage and pain, evil and hatred, from a devil in torment, an animal that had come up from the bowels of hell itself and transcended death.

John Broughton forced himself to look and saw the fox tottering on its hind legs, front paws outstretched like fists being shaken at him. Its back was arched until its spine almost snapped. Curving backwards, it was screeching, then it fell into the shadows where it was lost to his view.

The others abandoned their instinctive wariness and cunning. They should have turned and fled; instead they flung themselves forward, leaping high into the air, then falling back – and leaping again. And again. But their hind legs were not powerful enough to springboard them to the height of the upper windows. Frenziedly jumping again and again, the vulpine pack deafened the stillness of an English autumnal night with their cry.

He fired the second barrel and saw another fox go down. It hit the gravel, rolled and tried to get up, but its broken back legs would not support its weight. It was screaming – just as Pamela might have screamed as she saw the speeding tanker bearing down upon her, Broughton thought. He heard her now in that fox cry as he ejected the spent cartridges and loaded two more. Oh, God, he had to silence that bastard awful noise!

Both barrels fired simultaneously this time. He saw the shot ripping into the fur, raking it. Blood started to run but the fox was still screaming. The empty cases ejected, bouncing somewhere in the bedroom. Another double shot, this time lacerating the mask, the jaws dripping scarlet instead of yellow saliva. The nose was frothing with bubbles that formed and burst as the head fell back and rested on the ground. Those hateful eyes were still watching him when it died.

The room was thick with powdersmoke. It brought on a spasm of coughing. Loading, he was unable to believe that the foxes had not fed. Sighting another, he fired and threw it back, then moved on to the next one. He was shouting hysterically, cursing, yelling and shooting.

Finally he was out of cartridges and below him the drive was littered with fox bodies. Some were dead or at least not moving; others twitched and gurgled their last with blood-filled lungs. A slaughter, carnage where it had seemed impossible.

John Broughton closed the window. In a paroxysm of coughing, he fell back on to the bed with the still smoking twelve-bore clutched in his hands. They had come for him and he had slain them. Just ordinary foxes that had gone crazy, there was nothing supernatural about them. If this was the Corby Curse then it was not invincible. He just had to fight back. Kill or be killed.

After a time he went back downstairs, switched on the lights and entered the lounge. The brandy bottle was still on top of the cocktail cabinet; he poured himself a double measure and drank it right off. Just when the bastards thought they were winning he had shown them otherwise, taught them a lesson, he laughed aloud. Then he fell silent as a sobering thought crossed his mind.

The poison had not killed either the rats or the foxes. His victory had been but a skirmish. Out there in the moonlit woods a host of carnivores waited, thirsting for the flesh and blood of the one who had defied the ancient laws of these Corby lands.

The final encounter was about to begin.

17

Jill Shank cooked breakfast as a formality, a routine that she was not prepared to break because of her husband and son. They had to eat something even if they didn't feel hungry. They had to keep their strength up. But the smell of frying bacon was nauseating, and she wondered if they could have made do with cereal and toast.

Anxiously she glanced at the clock every few minutes. Five past seven. They should be back soon. *Oh, please God, let them come back*! She crossed to the window again and tried to see out through the rain-lashed pane. It was pouring outside, which made everything seem worse. She peered, wiped the glass with her hand, but it did not help. Listening, she could hear just the pattering of raindrops and the downspout leaking – probably the guttering blocked by a bird's nest, she reckoned. Going back to the stove, she moved the frying pan off the ring, still waiting.

Then she heard the chug of the old Land Rover and rushed to the door. Gordon was back, pulling in through the gate. *My boy's all right, too isn't he?* She felt instant relief as she saw Gary jumping down, his clothing sodden. She went back into the kitchen. Well, everything was fine right now; she had learned to live from hour to hour.

They were kicking off their muddy wellingtons in the porch, dropping their jackets on the floor. She looked up as they came into the room and saw how strained Gordon was, white-faced with black rings round his eyes. Like herself. He wasn't talking; nobody wanted to talk.

They ate in silence. Gary started school today, which meant transporting him down to the main road to catch the school bus into Stratford. Perhaps they all ought to go down, she thought; it wasn't safe to be apart. Stick together at all times — but that wasn't practicable when a gamekeeper had a job to do.

Empty plates, a second cup of tea. Only then did Gordon break the silence.

'*The bait wasn't touched*!' he whispered, wincing at his own words. '*Not only the foxes didn't eat it, but nothing else did, either. They . . . know*!'

Jill stared. 'That's impossible!'

'Yesterday I would have said so but now I've seen it with my own eyes. I'm going to spend the morning digging the deepest hole I can to bury the poisoned lights in. Really deep, because strychnine never dies. We've got the stuff all bagged up in plastic sacks. One bait after another untouched. And the pest control man claims that the rats aren't taking his bait, either!'

Staring at one another, toying with cutlery, they were afraid.

'Jill,' Gordon looked up and there was a pleading, a determination in his voice. 'I want you to go to your mother's and take Gary with you. And stay there. I don't want either of you on the Corby estate after today.'

'Not without you,' she snapped. 'I'd go right now but I'm not leaving any of my family *here*! Certainly we'll send Gary, he can go to school there with Claire and — '

'No, Mum!' Gary was close to tears. 'I won't go. Not without you and Dad.'

'Oh, *why* can't we all go!' She was choking back her tears. — 'This place is finished, Gordon. You know that as well as I do. There's no shooting left, the tourism trade is gone. Broughton's just clinging on but he can't avoid financial ruin. He'll be bankrupt before Christmas. You don't owe him anything — it's the other way round. Your job will be gone in a few weeks. Better to be unemployed and looking for another job than . . . *dead*!'

He dropped his gaze, knowing that she spoke the truth. It wasn't because of Broughton ... Jill would never understand. A gamekeeper run off the estate by the vermin he was supposed to control meant defeat, surrender. When you started a job you wanted to finish it. He loathed poison; it was indiscriminate, illegal, but it killed — everywhere else but on Corby ground.

'I'm thinking about it.' He pushed his chair back and stood up —, 'Maybe at the end of the week. I've got some clearing up to do first. But I want you to take Gary away, I'll join you at the weekend. That's a promise.'

'Then we'll all stay till the weekend,' she said, turning away. 'As I said, I won't go without you.'

Heads turned towards the rain-spattered window. A car was approaching down the track, and slowing.

'Here's the boss.' Gordon made for the door. 'I'll tell him that we're all pulling out on Saturday.'

John Broughton had fallen asleep just as dawn was creeping into the eastern sky. Physically and mentally exhausted, he slept heavily and was awoken just before seven by the rain drumming on the bedroom window. He stirred restlessly as he lay there and let the memories of last night seep back into his confused brain. It might have been some awful nightmare except that the Purdey on the bed beside him and the litter of spent cartridge cases on the floor told him it wasn't. It had all been horribly true. But those foxes had died, and that proved that if the Corby Curse really did exist then it was not invincible. Today the battle against the crazed creatures must continue.

He did not pull the curtains. He found the rain depressing and he would have to face it later. First, a bath and a shave, a change of clothes and then he would go and see how Gordon Shank had fared with the strychnine bait. If lead shot could kill these animals, and mink had been shot too, then surely poison would. His euphoria was tempered only by the memory of

Pamela's death; however much you had fallen out of love with somebody it was still a blow. The loss of his wife was only just becoming reality.

He dressed in a pair of cotton trousers and a flannel shirt, and wore his waterproof Barbour. Almost as an afterthought he fetched the gun from the bedroom and called in at the gunroom for another box of shells. Wherever he went, he would go armed; there was always the possibility of another shot at foxes. He relished that prospect now. The twelve-bore cradled under his arm, he let himself out of the front door.

And stood and stared in absolute disbelief. There should have been dead foxes lying on the drive and lawn. *But there were none*! There was not a vulpine corpse in sight on either the weedy gravel or the sun-browned lawn which was showing its first vestige of green. Neither blood nor fur. Nothing at all.

John Broughton trembled, feeling his spine begin to tingle, and with fingers that shook he loaded the gun. Barrels pointed towards the shrubbery, he waited. Gone was his confidence, his defiance of the Corby carnivores. A shrinking void in his stomach balled his guts. The bastards were playing tricks, he realized, pretending to be dead! But he had seen it all with his own eyes – the shotblasted bodies, the masks that streamed blood – heard the agonised screeching of fatally wounded animals; seen them lying stretched out. Feigning death! Slinking away as soon as he had returned to his bed! But no creature on this earth could live with those wounds.

They had.

Scared, he walked crablike towards the parked Subaru. His gun swung in a wide arc; but if he had failed to kill them before, what chance had he now? Oblivious of the pouring rain on his waterproof, he was still watching for them as he fumbled the car door open. He slid into the driving seat and propped the shotgun up on the passenger side, then switched on the wipers so that he could see. But there was nothing to see except dripping foliage weighted down by the wet.

Gordon Shank met him at the door and stood aside for him to enter. Jill and Gary looked pale and frightened. Everybody was frightened.

'Well?' There was no time for formal greetings, just a monosyllabic question. *Did they take the bait? I know they didn't but for Christ's sake tell me they did*!

'Nothing was touched.' The expected reply. 'No crows, nothing. I'm burying the poisoned meat as deep as I can dig.' *And you bloody well try to tell me to do otherwise*!

'They came last night.' Broughton spoke quickly. Too quickly. He saw the frightened glances of the woman and the boy. 'I shot 'em, four or five of 'em, I don't know for sure how many. Rolled 'em over, had 'em lying out there dead in front of the house. And this morning. . . .'

'They were gone.' Shank's head was bowed, his shoulders hunched. 'We have to face up to the fact that we can't beat 'em. That's why I'm leaving at the end of the week.'

Broughton nodded. He had been expecting this. Jill Shank's expression was defiant, there was no way anybody was going to stop them leaving. 'Okay.' He was trying to smile. 'I don't blame you. I'll have a month's pay-packet made up for you.'

'And you're staying on?' Gordon Shank looked at Broughton and read the hopelessness in his eyes. The man had lost everything: his wife, his fortune, his ambition. He had no reason to quit because there wasn't anything left for him.

'I'll be staying.' John Broughton turned towards the door. 'And . . . thanks for everything, Gordon. You, too, Jill, Gary.'

They watched him walk back to his car, a broken man. But he still had his pride. Which was why he would stay. And die.

The telephone was ringing when he walked back into the big house, a shrill screech that demanded to be answered or else it would scream all day. He lifted the receiver, aware that he still had his gun in his other hand.

It was the police. 'I'm sorry to trouble you sir.' A formality — Broughton was sure the policeman wasn't sorry at all, but probably annoyed because his call had not been answered immediately. 'I've had the post mortem report on your wife, sir. Perhaps you can shed some light on a mystery. She had been ... *bitten by snakes!*'

Broughton did not gasp 'snakes!' He was surprised, puzzled — but nothing was going to shock him, not after these last few weeks. His mind reeled; he could not cope with any more. *Does it bloody well matter now she's dead?*

'Are you still there, sir?'

'Yes, yes. Snakes, you say? I can't for the life of me imagine how that happened.'

'Neither can we, sir. We know there has been a lot of trouble with animals up at your place, but she was a good hundred miles from home. We can only conclude that she was carrying the reptiles in the car, possibly unknown to herself.'

Jesus, he knew Pamela wouldn't have gone within ten yards of a snake. There was an oblique accusation that *he* put them in the car, just as he released the rats out of his attic and drove the cattle over that German. *Murderer!*

'We shall have to delay the funeral pending the coroner's report, sir.'

'Oh, yes. I see. Well, I'm sorry I can't help you. Keep me informed, will you?' *No, don't.*

'I'll be in touch again shortly, sir. You aren't going away at all, are you?'

He stiffened. Was he under a kind of unofficial house arrest, being told to stay home until they had enough evidence to charge him? 'No, I'm not going anywhere, Inspector.'

God, it would be ironic if they proved a trumped-up murder charge, he thought. The Corby Curse would certainly have got him then. He pursed his lips, and went in search of the brandy bottle again.

The two gardeners had returned, which was surprising. Broughton stood in the bedroom window watching them as they walked across the lawn in front of the house. Now, he wondered, what the devil had they come back for?

They had chainsaws. The harsh whining became an angry drone then rose to a high pitch; ticked over, and started up again. They were cutting down the rhododendrons, sawing the bushes off at ground level, dragging them across to the middle of the lawn and piling them up. Working feverishly, they did not stop for a lunch break. Right on into the afternoon they heaped the sawn bushes into a mountainous structure, throwing on any branches they dropped. Of course, they were going to make a bonfire; there was no doubt about that.

After a while realization dawned. Pamela had wanted the rhododendrons cut down but he had adamantly refused. She was a wilful girl, and she had obviously telephoned these fellows whilst he was away and asked them to come back and clear the shrubbery. Any other time he would have gone berserk and they would not have got past the first bush. Now he didn't care. In fact it was a good idea. The foxes wouldn't be able to hide in there and watch him. It would open the place up a bit, let the daylight in. He should have agreed in the first place.

They were going to have some difficulty in getting the green foliage to burn, especially in the pouring rain, he thought. Perhaps they would leave it until another day, let the fresh growth wither and die. Or perhaps use paraffin. Whatever they did, it was a bit close to the house. He'd keep all the windows shut and, in any case, the place was in need of redecorating externally.

The men were finished now; instead of a mass of evergreens that obstructed the daylight and blocked the view, he could see right down to the river. He marvelled at the landscape, the home covert, Spion Kop on the horizon. Pamela had been right, and it was a kind of monument to her, a wide open space. And when the workmen burned the cuttings it would be like a funeral pyre. Damn it, he did miss her a little after all.

The older man went away and returned with a blue can, unscrewed the lid and began to splash its liquid contents all round the base of their edifice of vegetation. He took out a box of matches, struck one and tossed it at the heaped branches, turning to run as he did so. A surge of instant flame roared angrily and ran up the side of the rhododendrons. Hissing, struggling to catch, it sent up a column of dense smoke.

The smoke thickened and he caught only a glimpse of an orange tongue of fire through it. Billowing, swirling, eddying, hissing, it was trying to get a hold on the wet green wood and leaves.

John Broughton turned away. The view was lost now. Outside resembled a thick November fog that reached out for the house with wisping grey fingers. Well, at least those bloody foxes wouldn't be able to lie up in there any longer, and the stench would probably keep them away from the house for days.

God, he was tired, exhausted. He flung himself on the bed and closed his eyes. He wanted to sleep but it was impossible, those bushes were starting to burn properly now, hissing and crackling, the flames roaring as they dried out the branches. He coughed. Damn it, the smoke was getting in the house, seeping in through an open window downstairs, filling the bloody place!

He smelled it, tasted it. A fit of violent coughing had him sitting up, staring into the semidarkness of a smoke-filled bedroom, rubbing at his smarting eyes.

In shocked awareness, he realized that the gardeners had not returned, that those dense bushes that lined the lawn and drive had not been cut down. There had been no chainsawing, no heaped bonfire outside on the lawn. *But there were flames crackling somewhere close by and smoke was pouring into the bedroom. Corby House was on fire!*

He could feel the heat. It seemed to be coming directly from above. Barely able to see, he stumbled across the room and wrenched the door open. Smoke swirled on the landing as he ran for the stairs. It was clearer here, the fire was definitely up above. He went down to the hallway, unlocked the front door and staggered out into the wet night, only stopping when he was on the lawn where the blaze should have been and wasn't. Looking up, he saw the attic storey ablaze, sparks showering into the murky night sky like a macabre fireworks display. A crash as part of the roof fell in, released a pillar of fire, spreading, racing, hungry for timbers that were riddled with woodworm.

A thought crossed his mind as he stood there, a helpless spectator to the final destruction of his empire: Pamela's funeral pyre had become reality. There was no way Corby house was going to be saved, it would be razed to the ground.

And far away, up in the woods, the foxes had begun to howl again.

18

John Broughton had stood on the lawn most of the night watching Corby House burn. Hypnotized, transfixed, he had made no move to call the fire brigade because it did not matter any more. Flames grew in intensity, reaching up into the night sky, sizzling in the torrential downpour. Timbers crashed as a section of the roof caved in, sending a fountain of sparks spraying in all directions. The inferno was yet to reach its peak when he heard the sound of approaching fire engines.

Two engines, the crew unrolling their hoses, sprayed foam on the blaze. A police car followed, officers mingling with the fire-fighters. They ignored the lone spectator; perhaps they had not noticed him yet, he thought.

'Are you all right?' It was Gordon Shank, his Barbour coat still damp from yesterday's work in the wet, his face an eerie orange glow in the reflection of the fire. 'God, you can't stand out here in your pyjamas, you're saturated!'

Broughton glanced down at himself, aware for the first time that his gaudy night attire clung wetly to his body. Maybe he was cold, but if so he did not notice it. He felt like an automaton that was beginning to wind down. I just want to watch the end, he thought. I'm entitled to that. 'I'm all right.' He had to shout to make himself heard above the noise of the blaze and the hoses.

'What happened?'

'I don't know.' He didn't know and he didn't care. 'They'll put the blaze out but they won't save Corby House.'

'I think you'd better come back to our cottage. You can't stay here, you'll catch pneumonia.' The gamekeeper clutched his boss by the arm and began to pull him away. 'Good job I hadn't gone to bed. I happened to look out of the window and saw the sky lit up. I knew it had to be the big house. Come on, let's get you back. You won't do any good stopping here. Leave it to the firemen.'

John Broughton allowed himself to be led back towards the Land Rover, stumbling as he went.

'Just a minute sir!' A man had detached himself from

the group gathered by the engines, tall and imposing, almost arrogant in his manner, and Broughton knew he was a police officer even though he wore plainclothes. The voice seemed vaguely familiar, probably that inspector who had phoned yesterday with his innuendoes. 'Mr Broughton, isn't it?' The policeman's face was shadowed so that his expression was hidden.

You know bloody well it's me. Broughton waited, a pathetic pyjama-clad figure, his confidence drained. Closing his eyes briefly, he knew that he was at a disadvantage. *No, I didn't put snakes in my wife's car but I'm too bloody tired to deny it. I'll even admit it if you'll just let me sleep.*

'What time did the fire start, sir?' The policeman towered over Broughton, demanding, almost threatening.

'I've no idea.'

'Roughly?'

'Christ! An hour ago, perhaps.'

'I see. Did you notice where it started?'

'Upstairs. In the attic. Probably the rats gnawed through the wiring.' *Those same rats that you think I kept penned up there and released to kill that woman and her brat.*

'Possibly. But we can't surmise at this stage. The experts will be able to tell when they go through the ashes. You didn't phone for the fire brigade right away, did you, sir?' The head was thrust forward, the question carried the impetus of an accusation.

'The phone's in the house.' John was exhausted and had to lean on his companion. 'I wasn't going back inside.'

'You could have gone to the keeper's cottage and raised the alarm.'

'But I didn't, did I?' Calling on all his reserves, he stopped himself saying: Why don't you charge me, arrest me, and get it over with? That's what you want, isn't it? 'Look, I just need to sleep. Call me later. I'll be at the keeper's house.'

'We'll be in touch.' The policeman turned and strode back towards the firemen. He was abrupt, angry because the man who owned these extensive grounds and the fine house which was crumbling to ashes had defied him.

'Come on,' Gordon Shank said, and slipped his arm around Broughton's shoulders to help him into the Land Rover. And for the first time he felt genuine pity for his boss.

'We *can't* let him stop on here on his own!' Jill Shank voiced what they had both been thinking for the past few hours.

Upstairs John Broughton was still sleeping on the bed in Gary's room. He had slept since they carried him up the stairs at four a.m. yesterday morning. Thirty-six hours and he had barely stirred, oblivious to the bath and clean pyjamas they had provided him with. Jill had wanted to call a doctor but her husband had said that the boss would be okay – just exhaustion, and the only known cure was sleeping it off.

A policeman had called, then gone away. Doubtless the law would be back. Statements, questions: they seemed very determined, the Shanks thought.

Jill had taken Gary to Stratford and put him on a train to her parents'. She and Gordon would follow at the weekend. At least, that had been the original idea.

'We're leaving at the weekend.' Gordon Shank turned away as he answered her, afraid that she might notice the lack of conviction in his expression; the doubt, the uncertainty. She detected it in his voice. *No, we won't be leaving because of John Broughton. He needs us. He doesn't have anybody else.*

'It would be on my conscience if we did.' Jill sat down. 'He's weak, exhausted. And he's just lost his wife.'

'Look.' Her husband turned to face her. 'Broughton is a millionaire, he doesn't have to lodge in a gamekeeper's cottage, whether we're here or not. He can afford to book in at the best hotel in the country and live there for the rest of his life if he fancies it.'

'No, he can't.' She lowered her voice. 'Because he's broke. He hasn't got two pennies to rub together now. He's probably bankrupt.'

'He'll get a big pay off from the insurance over the fire. He doesn't have to try to sell the place now. He can rent the farms to his tenants, sit back and enjoy life. Providing, of course, the insurance company pays him!'

Their eyes met and they read each other's doubts, suspicions. Jill glanced up at the ceiling almost guiltily in case their unwanted guest had overheard them.

'I'm sure Mr Broughton wouldn't do a thing like that,' she whispered.

'I don't think so but I'm not sure.' He paused, then went on, 'You told me yourself that things weren't good between him and his wife.

'So don't fall for the grieving part. He's okay, he's a survivor in any situation. We don't have to stop here and play nursemaid to him.'

'I owe it to Pamela, she was a good friend. And not many ladies in her position befriend a keeper's wife, do they?'

'Oh, Christ Above!' He sighed and shook his head, 'You fell for it hook, line and sinker. She was lonely and missed her friends in London. She was scared to hell here, like the rest of us. So she used to come here because there was nowhere else to go. Don't be fooled by it. Don't misunderstand me, either; she liked us, but if there had been somebody – middle class she could have made a friend of, I don't think she would have been sitting in this room drinking our tea. Be realistic, Jill. You wanted to leave yesterday, now it's you who's trying to stop us going!'

'Gary and Claire are safe. If we stop around the house and don't go up into the woods, we'll be all right. It's only in the short term until Mr Broughton has made up his mind what he's going to do.'

'Well, we can't make any plans until we know exactly what *his* plans are,' he said. 'Let's wait and see. Don't let's make any rash decisions.'

Just after eight o'clock that evening they heard movements in the room directly above, then footsteps out on the landing and coming down the stairs. They looked at each other, tense with expectancy. Their decision was about to be made for them.

John Broughton looked somewhat comical in the tight-fitting clothes which Shank had put out for him, the stretched plus twos, the working shirt that threatened to pop its buttons at any second, the jacket about to burst its shoulder seams. He was white-faced but recovered, refreshed, the old determination back in his smile. Confidence, he had often proclaimed, bred success. And when you hit rock bottom there was only one way to go – up!

'Thanks.' He accepted a mug of tea which Jill set down on the table in front of him. 'I take it there was nothing left of the house?'

'Just a burned-out shell,' Gordon replied. 'I went up and had a look at it this morning.'

'Too bad.' He sipped his tea and looked thoughtful. 'But it's not the end of the world. I mean, I don't have the problem of selling now, do I?'

The Shanks exchanged glances.

'I don't have anywhere to live.' There was no self-pity in Broughton's voice, just a statement. 'Not round here, anyway. I don't want to go back to London. I suppose . . .'

'It's *your* cottage,' Shank replied. 'You can stay in it if you want after we've gone. If you would be good enough to let us hang on until the weekend like we said . . .'

'I don't want you to go.' Broughton smiled. 'You're a good keeper, Gordon, and I'd be hard pressed to find another of your calibre.'

'Thank you, but – ' It was a long time since Gordon Shank had blushed.

'No "buts" about it, I want you to stay. Please!'

'But there isn't any shoot left. The poults were killed, the animals have gone crazy and . . .'

'There are plenty of wild birds in the wood, you know that as well as I do. Enough to organize shoots on a limited basis. Reduced rates, but it'll mean money in the kitty. And in this age of chequebook shooting, a lot of sportsmen will pay for the privilege of shooting wild birds rather than semi-tame ones that don't fly above head height. And you've got to admit, Gordon, our pheasant are certainly *wild*!'

'They are that.' Gordon Shank was fidgeting, sensing Jill's eyes on him. Staying here was one thing, he thought. Remaining as gamekeeper on an estate where death was an almost everyday occurrence was quite another. 'If it wasn't for the Corby Curse . . .'

'Corby Curse be damned!' Broughton slapped his thigh and laughed. 'You don't really believe in that poppycock, do you?'

'Don't *you*?'

'I bloody well don't! I've given it a lot of thought lately and I reckon I know what's behind the animals' behaviour. Some kind of rabies-type disease, a virus that can be picked up by animals and birds alike and it sends them crazy.'

'Then why haven't they got in on the surrounding farmland?'

'Because it has, for some reason, broken out *here*, on the Corby estate. It will spread, make no mistake about that. But it had to start somewhere. We're just the unlucky ones. And those stupid villagers have leapt on the bandwagon, spouting about the Curse. The press have blown it up out of all proportion. All right, the creatures are dangerous. Because they are sick, *not* bewitched. And they didn't take the bait because they're hungering for their own kill. You got the crows, we killed the mink. Those foxes I shot were so diseased they survived to die a lingering death elsewhere. I remember once, some years ago, rolling over a bolting rabbit that obviously had myxomatosis. It got up after the first barrel, so I downed it again with the second. And it jumped up and continued running. And we never found it. In the end these creatures are just going to die. I want you to stay, Gordon.'

'I don't know.' The keeper shook his head and did not dare look at his wife. She might have changed her mind yet again!

'I'm offering you double wages, Gordon.'

He stiffened. Money was something he had never had in quantity. A living wage plus perks: rabbiting money, mole-catching in February, free firewood. A lifestyle, that was what he worked for, the freedom to roam the woods and fields – except that things had changed and now a keeper was under pressure and spent the spring and half the summer in the incubating and brooder shed, a kind of artificial poultry farmer. A keeper's children were deprived of a lot of things that other kids took for granted. Gamekeeping was selfish, doing what *you* wanted to do and damn your family. With a factory job you had money and leisure time, twice what you earned rearing pheasants for wealthy sportsmen. Unless you were suddenly offered double wages to do the job you were already doing. You could put up with an awful lot then. Even the Corby terrors, if your kids were safely out of the way.

He found the courage to look at his wife. Their eyes met; hers said: 'It's up to you, of course, but I'm for staying. Like I said, we owe it to the Broughtons, especially Pamela. We might help to save his bacon.'

He nodded and spoke in a voice that trembled. 'All right. We'll stay on. But on a week-to-week basis, and we're free to go at any time without working our notice if we change our minds.'

'Fair enough.' Broughton's tenseness drained out of him and his smile was one of relief. 'I am most grateful to you both. As I said, I think all this business has to come to an end soon. It's a disease plus a lot of unfortunate coincidences like my wife's accident and the fire. But if we stick it out then things are bound to improve. Now, there's only a month to go until the start of the pheasant-shooting season. I'm going to try and book some parties and sell three days in October. And if we up the beaters' pay I don't think we'll have any trouble with them.'

Gordon Shank had his doubts. For John Broughton it was a last desperate throw. A gamble with life and death.

September was virtually trouble free on the Corby estate. The wildlife made itself scarce, keeping to the woods and deep undergrowth, Gordon Shank decided. He almost believed Broughton's theory.

He used the Land Rover to feed the woodland rides, tipping corn from the safety of the vehicle without getting out. Work was easier: no traps or snares, Nature left to her own devices. The crunch would come when the first shoot began. It was a day he was dreading, but if everything went all right then he and Jill would stay on and the children could return from her parents'.

John Broughton was busy. He spent very little time in Corby. The coroner's court reached a verdict of death by misadventure on Pamela. The question of the snake-bites was raised but nobody had found any adders, dead or alive, on that stretch of motorway.

The police questioned Broughton about it. But now their efforts were concerned with the fire. They were suspicious because he had not called the fire brigade and his own financial circumstances provided a motive for arson. But suspicion was not proof. All the same, the insurance company were dragging their heels. Like the police, they were not satisfied.

Meanwhile, he concentrated on getting enough sportsmen together to provide three shooting parties. The press had become bored with the Corby Curse. It had reached a climax with the fire and then gone dormant. Once out of the headlines it was forgotten; sport was at a premium and within a week John had filled the remainder of his vacancies.

Alternative preparations had to be made now that the big house was no longer available to accommodate the shooting men. A five-star hotel was the base. On arrival the guests were wined and dined, breakfast the following morning, a sandwich lunch during a break in the shooting, and back to their hotel for dinner, departure on the third day. A set charge of fifteen pounds for every pheasant shot should cover everything, he calculated, and show a good profit. A hundred-bird day was anticipated for six sportsmen – nine grand gross. Times three for the month. And the same could be arranged for November, December and January. His optimism bordered on exuberance.

Gordon Shank was not so sure. For him it was a tense time of waiting. And perhaps for the Corby carnivores, too.

19

The shooting party assembled at the keeper's cottage and drank coffee served by Jill Shank in the brooder shed, which had been specially cleared for the occasion. At midday they would eat sandwiches in here whilst the beaters ate theirs outside. Fortunately they had never enjoyed the comfort and hospitality of the big house, Shank reflected; it was a case of what you had never had, you never missed. Everything was improvised, hopefully, cunningly camouflaged.

There were six guns in all, including John Broughton dressed in his familiar tweed shooting suit with plus twos tucked into long stockings. Gordon scanned them briefly; mostly the *nouveaux riches* taking up a fashionable sport. It might have been golf, but perhaps pheasant-shooting carried a greater status symbol. Expensive guns – he noted two Purdeys and a Westley Richards being displayed ostentatiously – fashionable clothing. Everything that money could buy except experience. Probably most of them had been to a shooting school and learned to hit clay pigeons, but today they would be put to the test. High pheasants were a match for any marksman. At least, Gordon hoped so. There were plenty of birds in the wood. He had sat in the safety of the Land Rover yesterday evening, listened to the cocks noisily going up to roost. If the beaters did their job then there would be sport for all, *if* these men could hit the birds that were flushed over them.

A face he recognized – it took him a minute or two to place it. The tall fellow with the short clipped moustache and sombre expression. Of course, Tattershall. Ex-army. Gordon remembered him coming to shoot at Manley, a man who shot five days a week on invitation because he was reputedly one of the best shots in Britain. Taciturn, you never tried to strike up a conversation with him, but he was of the calibre that every gamekeeper loved to have amongst the guns because he swelled the count at the end of the day.

Gordon scrutinized the beaters. Mostly regulars, but today they seemed cowed, huddling together as if seeking safety in numbers. Because they *knew*, would not have turned up except for the double rates Broughton was paying. Old Jukes, eighty last birthday, was gnarled and bent, but he would beat through the six-foot-high bramble patch if there was likely to be money in his arthritic hand at the end of the day. Young Sid Dale, wearing a floppy ex-WD camouflage hat to hide his punk haircut, was mainly interested in the beer at lunch break. Thompson from Leamington had his yellow labrador dog which he boasted had the best nose in the country – and no wounded pheasant had ever eluded him. Shank recognized a few from the village, others he didn't – friends of friends, here for the money because you didn't get beaters' wages like that anywhere else in the country except maybe at Sandringham.

Everybody was tense, shuffling their booted feet and mutely cursing the guns for wasting time over coffee. *Let's get on with it and get finished.*

'Ready, keeper?' Broughton turned away from his guests with a show of authority because they expected it, formal, commanding. 'We'll drive the home covert first.'

Which had all been planned days ago, Shank thought, as he signalled to the beaters. A tractor and trailor loaned by Farmer Yates transported them up the hill to the edge of the wood, the Land Rover in the lead with Gordon at the wheel. The keeper had thought about bringing his gun along but he decided against it. Some shooting men frowned upon a keeper carrying a gun when they were paying fifteen pounds for every pheasant shot. Not that he would have fired at pheasants; they were for the waiting line of guns. As they came in sight of the big wood, still dense with foliage that had barely a hint of autumn colouring in it and shrouded by an early mist that would not clear until the sun broke through, he shivered and regretted that he had not come armed.

'Right.' It was his turn to be commanding now that he was away from John Broughton, addressing the beaters as they climbed down from the trailer. Jukes was getting too old for the job. It was time somebody told him. His body bowed, he had to straighten up slowly and painfully. 'Line out, ten yards apart, and keep in line. I don't want to see anybody forging ahead or dawdling. Dale, you act as a stop. Go on, man, get going!' The arrogant bastard, he didn't like taking orders, slouching away down the side of the wood to position himself ahead of the others. 'Billy, you're stop on the far side. Go on, get moving, you've further to go than anybody else.'

With a general air of reluctance the beaters had turned up, something which Gordon had been doubtful about, but their heart was not in the job. Which, he supposed, was only to be expected.

Now they had to wait ten minutes; he checked his watch. Broughton would be drawing the peg numbers at the opposite end of the home covert, making sure that every gun knew which was his stand, and checking his own watch, too, waiting for the keeper's whistle for the drive to commence.

Gordon blew his whistle, an old Acme Thunderer which had been a regular police issue a quarter of a century ago. Glancing to his right and left, he saw the line of men and youths move forward, plunging into the bracken and undergrowth. Sticks tapped on tree trunks, beat at briar bushes; hollering, each beater had his own particular call. But today there was no enthusiasm, rather a half-hearted noise as though they feared to be heard, were frightened of the skulking birds they were trying to put on the wing.

Twenty yards, thirty. The mist, the stillness was eerie. The beaters were hanging back, for once determined not to lose sight of their nearest colleague.

'Get on!' the gamekeeper yelled, his shout muffled by the mist, which seemed to be thickening rather than dispersing. 'What's the bloody matter with you?'

With defiant expressions, the advancing line closed up as each man sought company, afraid of being alone. Something ran through the bracken and bolted for some adjacent brambles. A rabbit. At least *it* was scared.

A sudden *cock up, cock-up* sounded harsh and resonant, and there was a brief glimpse of a long-tailed bird striking powerfully up through the trees, going forward. A minute or so later the beaters heard the single shot from in front of them. A double or a salvo would have heralded a miss. One shot meant a second was not needed because the bird was dead. Gordon had long ago learned to read the scene up ahead of him with his ears and knew the formula. The bird was gaining height, going like the wind, the high pheasant that sportsmen demanded.

Then came a sudden rush of wings, an explosion of birds up ahead which had run on and grouped, knowing that the beaters were advancing and accepting that they had no choice but to fly. Wingbeats whirred and slapped their way up through leafy boughs; one after another, a constant steam of pheasants becoming airborne, seeking safety in flight. More. And still more.

'Fucking hell!' Gordon cursed. The last thing you wanted was to flush a big lot of pheasants, you did your best to put them up singly or in pairs, providing a steady steam over the guns. It was as though every bird in the home covert had gathered together, a kind of great escape: *They can't shoot us all.*

The beaters stood there anticipating the inevitable volley of shots, almost cringing in the bracken, they were frightened because they had never known so many birds break cover together, not even in the days when they had beat out Soar Wood over on the other side of the Corby boundary, where shooting had taken place when these lands were a sanctuary for wildlife. The men had deserted the Soar shoot for money; now they regretted it for there was evil here. They smelled it in the damp air, felt its clammy misty fingers touching them. They wanted to flee – damn the money and the beer. But it was too late because they were here.

And then they heard the shooting. Shot after shot, expensive ejector guns enabling their owners to reload fast. The guns were shooting as quickly as they could push another couple of cartridges into the breech.

Something was wrong. Gordon knew it, was certain of it. That big flush of birds would have cleared the shooting line in less than half a minute because the pheasants were bunched. Somebody like Tattershall might have managed to reload and shoot twice. A less accomplished marksman would have managed no more than a quick double after his initial shots. *But the shooting was still going on, rapid fire, incessant. The meadowland that sloped down to the river echoed with gunfire. And now there was shouting, screams of terror, coming from up ahead.*

Tallershall had killed the first cock bird well out in front as it rocketed out of the wood. A textbook shot; the bird had folded up, dead in the air, somersaulting, plummeting to bounce on the soft grass. It lay on its back, twitching until the nerves were spent, its splendid colourful plumage ignominous in death.

Somebody further down the line shouted, 'Good shot, sir!' But the tall man was unmoved. He expected it of himself, he would have been annoyed had he missed or had to use his second barrel. There was a click as the ejector threw out the spent and smoking empty case. Reloading, he took up that deceptively relaxed stance, waiting for the next bird over.

A good start, John Broughton thought. There was nothing like a brilliant kill to encourage the others. There would be plenty of birds, the shooting would be fast and furious.

At first he thought it was a flock of those damned crows coming over the tall oaks. Except that they were flying too fast and had long tails. Staring in disbelief, he cursed, blaming the beaters for rushing through the undergrowth and causing the pheasants to break all together. There must have been eighty or a hundred of the birds, towering to clear the trees. They would be very high by the time they reached the waiting guns. Then, to his horror, Broughton saw the oncoming pheasants start to dip, to lose height. Christ, no! It had to be an optical illusion; they would not plane down towards a line of shooters – even pheasants were not that stupid in spite of their suicidal tendencies in other respects!

But it was true. The birds were no more than ten yards up and still losing height, seeming to split into half a dozen different groups, arrowing towards those who stood with shotguns at the ready.

'I don't bloody believe it!' Broughton's gun was at his shoulder. He squeezed off a shot at the birds coming directly for him.

He saw feathers billowing, two shapes falling, a double kill because the pheasants were so tightly packed. He squeezed the second trigger and knocked another out, then he was flinging himself flat on the ground as they dived in at him.

He felt his hat knocked from his head by a feathered body that missed him by inches. Fluttering birds were alighting, coming at him like enraged cockerels in a farmyard. Kicking out at them, he threw up his arm to protect his face as one flew at him, screeching. Somehow reloading with one hand, he blasted three more into obscurity at a range of no more than five yards. Reloading, he shot again. Blood and feathers were strewn across the grassland; shotblasted unrecognizable corpses lay everywhere. And to his right and left there was continuous panic-sticken firing.

Tattershall had blood streaming down a gashed cheek where a set of spurs had raked him. The tall man was standing on a dead bird in a macabre posture of victory, driving the attacking pheasants back by his sheer speed with a gun. He was slaughtering them on the ground, an unsportsmanlike act of which he had never been guilty before.

The gun next to him was down with a cluster of

feathered, crazed killers on him, pecking his face, lusting for that greatest delicacy of all: human eyeballs. He was screaming for help but everybody was too busy trying to defend themselves. Pheasants jumped and hurled themselves at their sworn enemy, man, caring not whether they were blasted or clubbed by the guns because there were plenty more to take their places. Their harsh calls were interspersed with shots. It was a kamikaze battle which they could not possibly win.

At last the surviving pheasants took to the wing and retreated to the safety of Spion Kop. Shots followed them, dropping one bird. It was only wing-tipped and legged it strongly for the nearest hedgerow. Men were picking themselves up, inspecting their wounds, using handkerchiefs as temporary bandages. They all turned their eyes towards John Broughton, cursing and blaming him because he was their host and in their anger and fear they needed a scapegoat.

'What the deuce happened?' Tattershall was limping towards Broughton, dabbing at his face with a handkerchief that was now bright scarlet. 'This is crazy, absolutely unbelievable. And I, for one, am not stopping a minute longer! Not only will I not pay a penny for this outrage but I shall be phoning my solicitor. There will be considerable damages, I can promise you that!'

A young man was sobbing, his gun lying forgotten in the dewy grass, and when he pulled his hand away from his face the onlookers recoiled in horror. A bleeding eye hung down by a single sinew.

Frightened, enraged, all of them converged on Broughton. And at that moment they heard terrified screams coming from the big wood fifty yards in front of where they clustered.

The punk was running towards the bloodied shooters, hatless now, his multicoloured Mohican hairstyle in full view. Gesticulating wildly, he yelled: 'Mr Jukes . . . *the foxes have got him*!'

Broughton shook off Tattershall's angry clutching

hand and pushed him to one side. Sprinting to the wood, he reloaded his gun as he went. Nobody was following him – he did not want them to. It was foolishness to go in there, he knew. He should have fled back to the gamekeeper's cottage; even further. But he went into the wood all the same, following the main ride.

Shouts and screams were coming from all directions, bodies were crashing through the dense undergrowth. A man emerged from cover, staggering, a hideous wound in his thigh from which blood was pouring. Broughton ignored him. He had to find Shank. And Jukes. And get them all out of here.

A frightening shape bounded on the track, the lithe, powerful reddish-brown body with pointed ears and a bushy tail. Its jaws slavered and dripped blood. Fresh human blood. Broughton fired from the hip, discharged both barrels simultaneously and saw the fur blow apart. A hole the size of his fist jetted out scarlet fluid. *Got you, you fucker*!

The fox staggered, went down and kicked wildly. Broughton skirted it, left it there. It might die but he doubted it. He had seen it all before; it was like watching the same film for the second showing – he knew what was going to happen next. And that made it doubly terrifying.

Beaters were fleeing in every direction. He shouted at them but they either did not hear him or else his cries went unheeded. '*Get out of the wood*!' Which they were attempting to do, anyway, so he was wasting his breath.

Gordon Shank came into view, his beating stick and thick cudgel in his hand. He seemed unharmed except for a scratch across his forehead which might have been caused by a briar. He pulled up when he saw Broughton, and wiped his hand across his eyes.

'Jukes?' Broughton whispered.

'Back there.' The keeper jerked a thumb. 'No good . . . nothing anybody can do . . . just try to save yourself. I think all the others are clear.'

Holding on to each other, Gordon Shank and John Broughton staggered from Corby Wood out on to Yates's meadow. Distant figures everywhere – some helping others, some walking or staggering – were all heading away from the home covert, glancing back fearfully as they went.

But there was no pursuit. Nothing moved. There was not a sign of either pheasants or foxes. Because the beasts of the wild had won the day, vanquished their hated enemy who had betrayed a centuries-old pact, and that was sufficient. Birds and animals had slunk back to their rightful kingdom to savour their bloody victory.

20

John Broughton sat staring at the kitchen wall in the keeper's cottage. He had been subconsciously counting the latticed patterns made by the late evening sun through the window. They elongated, faded, then were gone all together. Like the Shanks. He had not attempted to prevent them leaving this time. There was no point in trying because this was the finish, no two ways about it.

The curse had won, he had to concede that. He had given up trying to find logical explanations for his misfortunes, for the death toll. He had lost count of how many had died. Just old Jukes yesterday, probably because he was too arthritic to flee with the rest of them. But innumerable injuries. Everybody was threatening to sue him, and meaning it. Everything had collapsed: the sport, the tourism. He could not think of any other avenue of income.

And the bloody police wouldn't let up. They were the worst, he thought. Bastards! They knew when you were at your lowest ebb, and took advantage of it. 'We are still trying to discover how *snakes* came to be in your wife's car, Mr Broughton.' *They bloody well crawled in when the car was standing outside with the door left open.* 'There is no trace of rats gnawing through the wiring in the attic and starting the fire. We'll be back to talk to you again tomorrow.'

The inspector was smirking, confident of breaking him down. Why don't you just make a confession, Mr Broughton, he seemed to be asking. Arson and *murder*.

Like everybody else, John Broughton wanted to leave Corby, didn't ever want to see the place again. Bankrupt me, and I'll maybe get a job gamekeeping, he thought; no money, but at least I'll be able to carry a gun and I know how to run a shoot.

He wanted to return to London but the police had requested him to remain – a kind of house arrest. He sat there in the dark, hit rock bottom and knew that the only way from now on was *up*.

That was when he really became angry, his smouldering fury about to burst into flames. The animals were responsible for this, whichever way he looked at it. A bunch of wild creatures had destroyed him, eroded his empire, brought death and destruction and now degradation. Just himself left, and that would not be for long.

He listened. Silence except for the wind, which was strengthening. There were always gales around the time of the equinox. The foxes weren't howling, the bats no longer fluttered at the windows, and there was not even the scurrying of a small rodent. Because they knew they had won.

And that was when he rose up out of the chair, shook his fist in the direction of Corby Wood. The fuckers thought he was beaten. They had let him live so that he could suffer the torment of the memories for the rest of his life. Oh, Jesus Christ, they didn't know John Broughton!

Revenge was all that was left to him. Bow out without so much as a whimper and he knew he would never be able to live with himself. One last desperate throw. An idea sprang to mind. There was no other way. God, they would pay for what they had done to him.

He pulled on his Barbour and went outside. The night was dry, with scudding clouds and just enough starlight to see by. And the wind would help, too, the canvas on the old Land Rover was flapping, threatening to tear itself free. Everything was right — perfect.

He went into the implements shed and shone his small pocket torch around until the beam rested on what he was looking for: a gallon drum of petrol which the keeper kept for topping up the vehicle when he had not got time to go down to the garage in the village. Broughton lifted it up; it was heavy, certainly almost full. Yes, for once everything was in his favour, the signs were right. He carried it outside, struggled to lift it up into the back of the Land Rover.

The drive up to the upper boundary of the home covert was steep and bumpy; he put the gears into four-wheel drive and felt the surge of power. There was no sign of life in the twin beams of the headlights, not even a rabbit hopping away into the undergrowth. The buggers were all resting up, he thought, confident that they had achieved what they had set out to do. Which was how John Broughton wanted it. When they realized their mistake, it would be too late.

He parked, then switched off lights and engine. The gale was tearing at the trees, baring the branches of their summer foliage a couple of weeks before the leaves would be ready to fall, like a blizzard in places, coming from the southwest.

There was an open space just inside the edge of the wood, a jungle of dead wild willow herb and bracken, briars and a few clumps of gorse. The perfect place.

He was hurrying now, almost feverish in his anxiety in case anything went wrong. The bastards were cunning but surely he had beaten them at the end. He struggled to carry the heavy can and had to wrest the rusted cap free when he reached that patch of wilderness. The petrol fumes made him heady, nauseated him, but he ignored them, splashing the fluid liberally on the dry vegetation, a line of ten yards and then back again, upending the canister and shaking out the dregs. He stood there, the night wind angry with him, trying to blow him over but he resisted it. It was nearly over now.

For one awful moment he thought that he had come without his matches, until he located them in the inside pocket of his thornproof jacket. Relief was followed by euphoria again.

He struck a match but the wind blew it out. *Fuck you*! But he couldn't have it both ways – he needed the wind to fan the flames. Cupping his hands, he used his unzipped coat to shield the flame from the wind. The brimstone head flared into life and he tossed it on to a clump of petrol-soaked wild willow herb.

The weeds seemed to explode. A sudden gush of fire leaped horizontally away from him, igniting the bracken and tearing on towards the gorse. A veritable fireball, a monster from hell, it raced to devour anything in its path.

John Broughton turned, and ran back for the Land Rover. He still carried the empty drum; it would have been too dangerous to leave it. That bloody inspector would doubtless sift through the ashes, trying to find the evidence which had eluded him so far.

He cursed himself for not having turned the Land Rover round beforehand. It was not easy, it took him half a dozen sweeps of the tight lock before he was facing the other way. Turning for one last look, he had to shield his eyes against the dazzling glare of that twenty-foot wall of fire which was sweeping down across Corby Wood, destroying all before it. Trees were already skeletal and blackened in the heart of the inferno, – which would not stop until it reached Yates's meadow. Perhaps only the river would halt it even then.

In his mind he heard the screaming of foxes trapped in their lairs, the smoke suffocating them where the flames could not reach below ground; pheasants roasted alive in their roosts; snakes frazzling in their hibernation hideaways, and only the dawn light would reveal the true extent of the devastation.

Driving slowly downhill, he was euphoric now because it was done and there had been no snags. It would make things right with Pamela, too; she had hated this place so he had destroyed it in her memory.

A sharp bend and then he would be back on level ground, cross the cattle grid and –

He had to brake sharply, slewing the vehicle in spite of the four-wheel grip, stopping within a foot of the white Metro which was blocking the track, facing him. Fucking idiots! A courting couple, doubtless, naked and screwing on the back seat.

The car's headlights flicked on, blinding full beam which pinned him back in his seat. He was aware that somebody was getting out and walking towards the Land Rover. He heard the door being opened, but all he could see was a tall silhouette which seemed vaguely, frighteningly, familiar behind the glare of the lights.

'Well, if it isn't Mr Broughton!' came the sarcastic tones of the glib police inspector as he thrust his angular face inside the vehicle.

Broughton was conscious of somebody at the rear of the Land Rover and the canvas flap being lifted up. There was a clanking as the empty petrol can dribbled the last of its pungent liquid contents from the uncapped lid.

'I must ask you to accompany us to the police station,' the inspector said smugly as he reached across and removed the key from the ignition.

Bestselling Thriller/Suspense

☐ Skydancer	Geoffrey Archer	£3.50
☐ Hooligan	Colin Dunne	£2.99
☐ See Charlie Run	Brian Freemantle	£2.99
☐ Hell is Always Today	Jack Higgins	£2.50
☐ The Proteus Operation	James P Hogan	£3.50
☐ Winter Palace	Dennis Jones	£3.50
☐ Dragonfire	Andrew Kaplan	£2.99
☐ The Hour of the Lily	John Kruse	£3.50
☐ Fletch, Too	Geoffrey McDonald	£2.50
☐ Brought in Dead	Harry Patterson	£2.50
☐ The Albatross Run	Douglas Scott	£2.99

Prices and other details are liable to change

ARROW BOOKS, BOOKSERVICE BY POST, PO BOX 29, DOUGLAS, ISLE OF MAN, BRITISH ISLES

NAME...

ADDRESS...

....

....

Please enclose a cheque or postal order made out to Arrow Books Ltd. for the amount due and allow the following for postage and packing.

U.K. CUSTOMERS: Please allow 22p per book to a maximum of £3.00.

B.F.P.O. & EIRE: Please allow 22p per book to a maximum of £3.00.

OVERSEAS CUSTOMERS: Please allow 22p per book.

Whilst every effort is made to keep prices low it is sometimes necessary to increase cover prices at short notice. Arrow Books reserve the right to show new retail prices on covers which may differ from those previously advertised in the text or elsewhere.

Bestselling Fiction

☐ No Enemy But Time	Evelyn Anthony	£2.95
☐ The Lilac Bus	Maeve Binchy	£2.99
☐ Prime Time	Joan Collins	£3.50
☐ A World Apart	Marie Joseph	£3.50
☐ Erin's Child	Sheelagh Kelly	£3.99
☐ Colours Aloft	Alexander Kent	£2.99
☐ Gondar	Nicholas Luard	£4.50
☐ The Ladies of Missalonghi	Colleen McCullough	£2.50
☐ Lily Golightly	Pamela Oldfield	£3.50
☐ Talking to Strange Men	Ruth Rendell	£2.99
☐ The Veiled One	Ruth Rendell	£3.50
☐ Sarum	Edward Rutherfurd	£4.99
☐ The Heart of the Country	Fay Weldon	£2.50

Prices and other details are liable to change

ARROW BOOKS, BOOKSERVICE BY POST, PO BOX 29, DOUGLAS, ISLE OF MAN, BRITISH ISLES

NAME..

ADDRESS..

....

....

Please enclose a cheque or postal order made out to Arrow Books Ltd. for the amount due and allow the following for postage and packing.

U.K. CUSTOMERS: Please allow 22p per book to a maximum of £3.00.

B.F.P.O. & EIRE: Please allow 22p per book to a maximum of £3.00.

OVERSEAS CUSTOMERS: Please allow 22p per book.

Whilst every effort is made to keep prices low it is sometimes necessary to increase cover prices at short notice. Arrow Books reserve the right to show new retail prices on covers which may differ from those previously advertised in the text or elsewhere.

Bestselling General Fiction

☐ No Enemy But Time	Evelyn Anthony	£2.95
☐ Skydancer	Geoffrey Archer	£3.50
☐ The Sisters	Pat Booth	£3.50
☐ Captives of Time	Malcolm Bosse	£2.99
☐ Saudi	Laurie Devine	£2.95
☐ Duncton Wood	William Horwood	£4.50
☐ Aztec	Gary Jennings	£3.95
☐ A World Apart	Marie Joseph	£3.50
☐ The Ladies of Missalonghi	Colleen McCullough	£2.50
☐ Lily Golightly	Pamela Oldfield	£3.50
☐ Sarum	Edward Rutherfurd	£4.99
☐ Communion	Whitley Strieber	£3.99

Prices and other details are liable to change

ARROW BOOKS, BOOKSERVICE BY POST, PO BOX 29, DOUGLAS, ISLE OF MAN, BRITISH ISLES

NAME..

ADDRESS..

....

....

Please enclose a cheque or postal order made out to Arrow Books Ltd. for the amount due and allow the following for postage and packing.

U.K. CUSTOMERS: Please allow 22p per book to a maximum of £3.00.

B.F.P.O. & EIRE: Please allow 22p per book to a maximum of £3.00.

OVERSEAS CUSTOMERS: Please allow 22p per book.

Whilst every effort is made to keep prices low it is sometimes necessary to increase cover prices at short notice. Arrow Books reserve the right to show new retail prices on covers which may differ from those previously advertised in the text or elsewhere.

Bestselling Crime

☐ No One Rides Free	Larry Beinhart	£2.95
☐ Alice in La La Land	Robert Campbell	£2.99
☐ In La La Land We Trust	Robert Campbell	£2.99
☐ Suspects	William J Caunitz	£2.95
☐ So Small a Carnival	John William Corrington Joyce H Corrington	£2.99
☐ Saratoga Longshot	Stephen Dobyns	£2.99
☐ Blood on the Moon	James Ellroy	£2.99
☐ Roses Are Dead	Loren D. Estleman	£2.50
☐ The Body in the Billiard Room	HRF Keating	£2.50
☐ Bertie and the Tin Man	Peter Lovesey	£2.50
☐ Rough Cider	Peter Lovesey	£2.50
☐ Shake Hands For Ever	Ruth Rendell	£2.99
☐ Talking to Strange Men	Ruth Rendell	£2.99
☐ The Tree of Hands	Ruth Rendell	£2.99
☐ Wexford: An Omnibus	Ruth Rendell	£6.99
☐ Speak for the Dead	Margaret Yorke	£2.99

Prices and other details are liable to change

ARROW BOOKS, BOOKSERVICE BY POST, PO BOX 29, DOUGLAS, ISLE OF MAN, BRITISH ISLES

NAME..

ADDRESS..

....

....

Please enclose a cheque or postal order made out to Arrow Books Ltd. for the amount due and allow the following for postage and packing.

U.K. CUSTOMERS: Please allow 22p per book to a maximum of £3.00.

B.F.P.O. & EIRE: Please allow 22p per book to a maximum of £3.00.

OVERSEAS CUSTOMERS: Please allow 22p per book.

Whilst every effort is made to keep prices low it is sometimes necessary to increase cover prices at short notice. Arrow Books reserve the right to show new retail prices on covers which may differ from those previously advertised in the text or elsewhere.